THE LAST MIXTAPE

THE LAST MIXTAPE

Steve Matsumoto

CONTENTS

CHAPTER 1

P.S. HOW DID SHE
DIE ANYWAY?

The room was far neater than I usually left it. That's what happens when someone dies—people who don't know what else to do start cleaning like indentured servants. Washing dishes is much easier than offering someone genuine empathy, so sponges and dustpans often become the tools for those trying to comfort the bereaved. I ran my hand over the impossibly smooth chalkboard and admired the precision with which someone had bothered to align all the desks and chairs. I had my strengths as a teacher, but keeping an orderly classroom was certainly not one of them. Room 22 was in perfect order. My life was not.

Like the rest of the classroom, my desk had been meticulously organized. Gone was the chaotic heap of field trip permission slips, papers to grade, and memos from the front office; on this morning I could actually make out the surface of the desk. And right in the middle of that imitation wood grain veneer, a stack of carefully folded construction papers, the sight of which filled my heart with dread. I knew exactly what that stack of papers was, but I wasn't ready for it yet. I threw my messenger bag on my chair and figured *coffee first* might be the answer.

I never planned to become a teacher, but somewhere along the way, I realized that teaching wasn't a choice I'd made—it was simply who I was. My father had failed to fulfill my Japanese grandmother's immigrant dream of her son becoming a doctor, and by extension, I had, too. Apparently, teaching first grade didn't honor my ancestors. Still, it paid the bills, and I really enjoyed it.

Coffee required a trip to the faculty room. Since my classroom was at the far end of the hall, it was a long walk, and this morning it would take even longer. Usually, I could just stroll anonymously past the intermediate classrooms, but as soon as Myra Reiner heard my footsteps on the polished terrazzo flooring, she sprang to her classroom door. As she greeted me, it immediately alerted the other third and fourth grade teachers. Every single one of them wanted to hug me and invite me over for dinner. Sadly, these hugs were the most physical contact I had experienced with females in quite some time. By the time I got to the gym, I'm sure I smelled like a cocktail of middle-aged women perfumes.

Hugs and dinner invitations were definitely not Monday-morning protocol. While I was one of only three male teachers at the school—and the only one who wasn't balding—my presence didn't typically garner this level of attention. Sure, as the young guy on staff, I'd been on the receiving end of my fair share of proxy mothering—but nothing quite like this. Funny thing about workplace culture: your coworkers' kindness tends to increase in direct proportion to how recently your sister killed herself. At least, that's what I've found based on a relatively small sample size.

Before I could return to my classroom, I had to tolerate a few more awkward embraces accompanied by the obligatory and useless "Please let me know if there's anything I can do." Coffee mug in hand, I surveyed the pristine environment and wondered what went on in my absence. In addition to house cleaning, both the school counselor and principal paid a visit to my class. "Your teacher isn't out sick today. He's not at school because his younger sister is dead." Or whatever Jean told them in her fake therapist voice. I could picture the puzzled faces of Ellie Lamore and Kayla Murray as they sat on the rug trying to make sense of it. And what did they tell their parents when they asked, "What did you do at school today?" That had to make for some interesting dinner conversations.

After the thoughts, feelings, and emotions of class were appropriately processed, they were invited to create sympathy cards for their teacher. Horrific, unedited, six-year-old perspective sympathy cards that were now sitting in the middle of my desk. As much as I didn't want to look at them, I knew that I had to. I put my coffee down next to the stack of colorful cards, and picked up one featuring a picture of a female stick figure with curly hair. *This was not going to be easy.* More than the middle-aged mom hugs, reading these cards were about to bring Kelly's death right here into my classroom.

Keep in mind, this was still pretty early in the school year and at best, half the class was able to read. I'm sure helpful words like "S-I-S-T-E-R" and "K-E-L-L-Y" were written on the board for the card-makers to reference. Some students simply used pictures to illustrate their feelings, and it didn't help that my sister died during October when a wealth of Halloween imagery was still fresh in their minds.

Richie Blake opted for a card with gravestones, lots of gravestones, like a military cemetery amount of gravestones. Perhaps, in his mind, Kelly would start her after-life carefully selecting a final resting place, kind of like a first-time homebuyer. Other cards featured ghosts and skeletons, including a very anatomically correct one buried underground. There was even one skeleton marked with "x" at the end of the treasure map. Clearly, Chris Peng had imperfect knowledge of both sympathy cards and pirate lore. Each card I opened was more tasteless than the last, but how could I blame Richie, Chris, or any of them for trying? They were just innocent kids intersecting with me at the strange crossroads of emerging literacy and personal grief.

Their cards were shaped as much by their feelings as by their developing grasp of reading and writing. When students go from recognizing a language pattern in print to being able to use it themselves, there's an excitement in using that skill. It's like learning a secret that other people were in on and they typically go through a period of overusing it. Some of my students had just learned that not all sentences end in a period and that exclamation points add

4

excitement. That, combined with the fact that many first graders write in all capital letters, led to some very forceful condolences:

"I'M SORRY!"

"SORRY ABOUT KELLY!!"

"YOUR SISTER DIED!!!!"

Except, it wasn't spelled "SORRY," but "SOREE" or "SREE." The capital letters and inventive spelling added to the kidnapper ransom note charm.

I was doing a pretty good job holding it together until I got to the card created by Maddie Flores. She was the best writer in the class, used uppercase/lowercase letters perfectly, and didn't need any words spelled out for her on the chalkboard. One of the writing patterns she recently discovered was that notes and letters sometimes ended with a postscript. Her pink paper was creased neatly in half and beautifully adorned with flowers on the front cover. In her best printing, she carefully placed the words "Sorry about your sister" in the center of her design. I was genuinely impressed with Maddie's emotional maturity until I flipped the card open. Inside, three comically oversized tears fell from a frowny face above an inquisitive closing, "P.S. How did she die anyway?"—as if it were some overlooked footnote, barely worth mentioning.

I could picture Maddie's face beside my desk asking me this exact question like she was wondering what our next reading group book would be. She'd inquire with genuine curiosity and an inquisitive smile, the gap left by her missing baby teeth only adding to her sincerity. Even if she could read at a third grade level, how was she supposed to know the social etiquette of tragedy—and how was I supposed to answer her?

The predictable, socially acceptable consoling from the adults was manageable, but nothing prepared me for the brutal honesty and rawness of my students' reactions. Adults say, "I'm sorry for your loss," which sounds like you misplaced your car keys. Kids say, "Your sister's dead," which quite frankly is a more accurate assessment of the situation. Whatever I expected on my first day back at school, it certainly wasn't crudely drawn pictures of my younger sister's skeleton sketched in scented markers.

I looked down at the frowny face in Maddie's card and felt the same three giant teardrops welling in my eyes. *My students hadn't even arrived yet and I was already crying!* I brushed the wetness from my face with the palm of my hand and tried to regain control of my emotions with a long inhale. No use. A wave of sadness hit me, followed by a flood of guilt. The students and faculty of Greenridge Elementary had reached out and wrapped me in their arms, yet all I felt was self-conscious about all the attention.

Suicide carries a stigma, and I couldn't shake the feeling that if they knew the truth—if they knew how she died—they wouldn't have embraced me the same way. At least that's what I told myself. I felt ashamed and embarrassed that my sister killed herself, like her death was a piece of spinach stuck in between my teeth for the whole world to notice. What can I say? Grief has a shade to fit any mood, and it finds the strangest ways to show itself.

A stray glance out the window revealed one of my students, Patrick Dean, holding his mom's hand, walking down Robertson

Street to school. Every day he showed up a half hour before the safety patrols opened up the front doors, just so he could be one of the first students to populate our building. Mrs. Dean had told me numerous times she tried to make her life easier by leaving for school later, but Patrick wouldn't have it. He just wanted to be at school, having a good time.

Christ, kid...me too.

CHAPTER 2

HALF GALLONS OF MILK

By the middle of November, school became the most normal thing in my life. There's nothing like teaching math students how to regroup tens and ones to take your mind off tragedy. Teaching became my distraction, my salvation. The problem was I could only stay at school so long; at some point Hank, the night custodian, would make me get in my car and go home. After school was a problem. The weekends were a problem. The supermarket was a huge problem.

Grocery shopping before going home to eat alone is sad. Grocery shopping before going home alone to think about your dead sister is cataclysmically sad. Somehow, I fell into a pattern of pain and solitude whenever picking out a half gallon of milk. Not because I was lactose intolerant, but because buying milk made me aware of time. Reaching for my weekly milk supply, I would look at the computerized timestamp under "Use by" date and wonder if *Future Me* would be better at that time printed on the carton. It would also bring about awareness that *Current Me* was absolutely not okay. Existential crises in the dairy aisle became a part of my weekly routine.

A couple weeks after Kelly's funeral, the support system had withered away. It's only natural for there to be a flurry of support immediately after someone close to you dies. In the beginning, people are coming over to your house, attending the funeral, cleaning your kitchen, and sending cards and flowers. At that point, everyone around the tragedy knows who you are, and you're kind of a celebrity. But like the business of elementary school, pretty soon everyone who came to the house or attended the funeral goes back to their regular lives. Now I was left with a trickle of Hallmark cards and memories of the worst week of my life.

All that could be done was enduring this stretch and letting time pass by. I wished it was like having a cold where I could sleep it off until I felt better, but I was wide awake for this nightmare. During the weekends, I'd play a game with myself. Seeing how much time can pass without a terrible thought popping in my head: the police at my mom's front door, seeing her lifeless body, the idea of her drowning herself with rollerblades on.

Even at the time, I knew that Kelly's funeral was necessary, but not for me. A funeral is kind of like a wedding ceremony in which you and Grief get married. All your friends and family come together in a church to witness the public pronouncement of your commitment to this particular pain and anguish. A month ago, I had no idea that I was about to enter into this arrangement. Now, my new lifelong companion moved into my one-bedroom apartment in West

Brunswick, New Jersey. Whenever I was home, it was just Grief and me: hanging out, playing Nintendo, eating cereal for dinner.

My apartment was furnished with leftovers from my parents' divorce, sad reminders of the childhood house I used to live in. The first thing my mom bought after my dad moved out was a circular dining table because our rectangular one with my dad sitting at the head was too hierarchical. (*Grounds for divorce? Furniture, your honor.*) I had inherited the less-democratic dinette set along with the coffee table my father built earlier in their marriage when money was tight. Simple in design, it was a giant, four-foot square sitting on top of a base forming an 'X'. It was way too big for my apartment, but it had lots of space to collect keys, magazines, coffee mugs, pizza boxes, and sunglasses.

I would sit on the couch with Grief and just think about my sister: memories, questions, possibilities, theories. We were like detectives working a case, searching for answers. All that was missing was the bulletin board with various pieces of evidence tacked up and strung together with yarn. While our investigation hadn't collected a lot of physical evidence, I still had the last mixtape my sister made me.

Before Spotify, Pandora, or burning CDs, there was the art of making mixtapes. Carefully curating and sequencing twenty-three songs on two sides of a ninety-minute cassette tape was both an art and a science. Kids today have no sense of the achievement that was hearing a chorus completely fade out followed by seeing your cassette reels freeze because you just ran out of tape, perfectly fitting in your last song. Once Kelly got to a point where I deemed her musical taste interesting, she and I started trading mixtapes, introducing each other to new bands and expanding our musical interests.

Our tradition consisted not only of sending each other a mixtape filled with awesome music, but also an accompanying letter, kind of like liner notes for a vinyl album. Each letter had to incorporate the title of every song on the tape in the exact order in which they appeared, seamlessly woven into the context of updating each other on our lives. If I wanted Kelly to hear "Raining in Baltimore" by the Counting Crows, I'd have to figure out some way to write about the weather in the Mid-Atlantic.

I don't remember how this ridiculous game started, but our enthusiasm for creatively constructing the tapes was matched only by the appreciative joy of receiving them. The best part was always the tangential detours the writer was forced to make to accommodate their musical taste. Inevitably, there was a song one of us had recently discovered that simply had to make the mixtape, even if its title had no business being in the letter. Try working "Who's Gonna Ride Your Wild Horses" into a letter about teaching first grade and hanging out in coffee shops because you know your sister needs that song in her life. The resulting bits of extraneous exposition were good, nerdy fun, reflecting the absurd sense of humor that Kelly and I shared. More than anything, though, receiving those tapes and letters from Kelly made me proud to be her older brother.

The last letter I received from Kelly was ostensibly about her sophomore year at the University of Vermont, but since her death it had taken on a completely new meaning. It may not have been her intention, but I considered it her suicide letter to me. Even though her tone and content reflected her typical quirky and upbeat self, her mix contained two or three songs that resonate much darker now. Grief and I were doing our best to attribute meaning that may or may not have been here.

For example, Kelly had introduced me to The Samples, so she closed this mix with their song "Nothing Lasts for Long," which she also cleverly connected to the end of her letter:

You'd probably like me to tell you more about life in Burlington, but I've got to go to class and this letter can't go on indefinitely because, as I'm sure you know, Nothing Lasts for Long.

Love, Kelly

One night, Grief and I were going over our case when the sudden, dramatic opening chord of "Nothing Lasts for Long" smashed through my bookcase speakers into my apartment. The music shocked and hypnotized me. As the lyrics began I knew every word, but somehow I was also hearing their truth for the very first time, as if their meaning was being tattooed upon my soul. The song is a wistful and melancholy retrospective, and at this moment I heard it as Kelly's personal goodbye to her older brother. It was as if Kelly, with unimaginable wisdom and foresight, personally placed this song in my life, knowing I would hear it after she left this world. I completely lost it. I broke down. I sobbed long and hard. For the first time in a long time, I cried myself to sleep.

A few days later, I thought I lost her mixtape and our connection to each other. Almost out the door on the way to school, I turned around to make sure I had my audio security blanket for the car. Surprisingly, it wasn't in the tape deck. Puzzled, I glanced around the room. I picked up a newspaper and then a belt off the coffee table but didn't unearth it.

Heat started to rise in my head and my heart was pounding against my chest. Shallow breaths of air rapidly pushed in and out of my lungs. Puzzled had quickly become panicked. *Where was this damn tape?* I darted around my apartment, searching every conceivable location. I got angry about losing the tape. I got angry about getting angry. I could feel that my frenzy prevented me from searching effectively and that made me even angrier. I thought I'd lost the last piece of my sister.

After some choice curse words and checking the freezer several times, I collapsed in front of the minimalist square coffee table. Only after sitting still and several deep breaths did I see the gray cassette wedged in between two couch cushions. It barely mattered. I knew I wasn't upset about a missing tape. It was 7:15 in the morning and I was mentally and physically exhausted. In case it wasn't obvious, Grief was a lousy roommate.

The missing mixtape incident demonstrated how raw and exposed my emotions were. Even when shielded by a thin veneer of happiness, at any point, I could be hanging on by a thread.

Obviously, it would take a few more half gallons of milk before things got better.

CHAPTER 3

HUGS & WINKS

Finding the mixtape had made a mess of my apartment. The day after trashing my living room like an eighties' hair band backstage, I surveyed the damage, not feeling incredibly motivated to clean up my temper tantrum. Distracted by other possible chores—there was also laundry to be done—I took the short walk down Palmer Street with a sack of dirty clothes and a pocketful of quarters. Slumped against a counter, I fixated on the storm of boxer shorts and t-shirts colliding on the other side of the glass door of the dryer. After half a cycle, my trance was broken.

"Are you using this?" someone asked, referring to the laundry cart near me.

"No, it's all yours." Turning to my right, I saw the most beautiful creature I'd ever seen at a public laundromat. Typically, the place was filled with shabbily dressed senior citizens with expressionless faces and felt like a purgatory of lost souls. The cart inquiry was lobbed from an attractive young female whose piercing eyes and shapely figure were a beacon of light and possibility among the unswept linoleum floor and din of the dryers.

Before I could say anything else, a huddle of older women burst through the door, arguing at each other in an Eastern European dialect. They continued yelling at each other—only stopping to point at various washers and then at each other; it seemed like they were determining who would wash whose clothes. I tried to picture my grandmother making a laundry date to wash her house dresses with five of her best friends. I looked up at Laundry Cart Girl and we shared a knowing glance and a half smirk.

"They all took the bus together," I offered, thinking this was as good an opening as any.

"From Odessa?"

"My thoughts exactly." I took Laundry Cart Girl's knowledge of one Ukrainian City as fact that she was smart *and* pretty. "It's actually ladies' night tonight. They're here for half-off fabric softener."

And with that, I got a warm and authentic laugh out of Laundry Cart Girl. She continued to smile as she worked. As I stole glances at her, I could see she was folding a series of thongs, and I allowed my imagination to run wild. I couldn't believe it. *Was I actually meeting my dream girl at Little Wash-N-Go?*

"I don't know about you, but I hate coming here. It's so depressing," she said and shook her head to emphasize the last two words.

"No doubt. It's like jury duty."

"More like the DMV." I laughed and recognized her better offering with a subtle finger point. *Oh my god this girl is adorable, smart, funny, and owns great underwear.* As I strategized a way to obtain her phone number, a figure much scarier than the Ukrainian grandmothers filled the front doorway of the laundromat.

He had to have been at least 6' 4", and his chiseled shape was stuffed into a black tank top and dark jeans. The jeans seemed to go on forever; this guy must have had like a fifty-inch inseam. His Levi's alone might have been taller than me. Taking ridiculously long strides, he parted the Ukrainians and crossed the room in seemingly three steps. He sauntered right up to Laundry Cart Girl; I knew it was all over before their lips even met.

"Hey, babe."

Of course Laundry Cart Girl has a boyfriend. No one is that complete of a package with that kind of undergarment inventory without having a boyfriend. I slowly retreated back toward my drying clothes and slumped into a bench, trying to make myself as small as possible. One of the Ukrainian women tapped me on the shoulder to indicate my clothes were done drying. I got no indication that she wanted to watch me fold my underwear.

While I struck out at the laundromat, my mailbox presented new possibilities when I got home. Examining the size of the letter, I could tell it wasn't another condolence card. While there was a familiarity to the handwriting of my address, I instantly recognized the artist of the cartoon in the corner of the envelope. It was a rough caricature, a little more than a stick figure drawing of a smiley-face female with long straight hair waving with one arm. It was the artwork of Allison Lockwood, a high-school classmate, whom I reconnected with at my sister's funeral.

Hello James,

How are you doing? That's actually a really silly question. If you're not doing so well, that's completely understandable. If you're doing okay, good for you. Well, I certainly seem to be babbling at the start of this letter.

(Here she included another cartoon drawing of herself with her arms extended in a "who knows" gesture.)

While the circumstances were awful, it was so good to see you at your sister's service. I've been thinking about Kelly a lot since then. Even though it's been a long time since she and I spent any time together, your sister was so special to me. I think about her coming over to my house to take care of the rabbits, make cookies, and draw together. I've been thinking a lot about you, too, and what you must be going through. I'm glad we got a chance to talk after Kelly's service.

Are you going to be at your mom's place over Thanksgiving? If you are, perhaps we could get coffee and talk some more.

Hugs & Winks,

Allie

I must have reread Allie's short note a dozen times. I carefully inspected her cartoon drawings, which had not changed that much since middle school. While the funeral was the first time I saw her since graduation, we were able to traverse a bridge there that had previously been built and never completely eroded away. Allie, Kelly, and I had an intricate history of being in and out of each other's lives; at the end of high school, Allie and I had completely fallen out of each other's orbits. But now, I was excited at the prospect of seeing her again. *Was I actually looking forward to something? Thanks-*

giving? My favorite holiday. Coffee with Allie? Sounds delightful. Sign me up for both!

For the better part of a month, I had no ability to look forward to anything, but today's mail correspondence changed everything. Allie's letter had cut off some of the ballasts that were holding me down and lifted me upward. I experienced a lightness I hadn't felt since Kelly went missing. My whole life lately had been focused on what was gone, but Allie's letter—and the mere prospect of having coffee with her—was right here in my hand. For the moment, possibility replaced pain, and instead of focusing on what I didn't have, I thought about what I could have.

Scanning the room, Grief wasn't in his usual spot on the couch. When I did finally spot him in the corner, he was actually being helpful for a change, gesturing toward the phone and saying, "Call her, you idiot!" Waiting through three or four rings, I was once again my middle-school self, nervous with anticipation and rehearsing phone etiquette in case Dr. Lockwood answered the phone. (Which was silly because Allie didn't live with her parents, but old habits die hard.) After one more ring, I was greeted by the warmth of the girl I met in fifth grade.

"Allie, it's James."

"Hi, James!" Her perky enthusiasm immediately lightened my heart. "I'm so glad you called. How are you?"

"Well...you know...," I responded too truthfully, effectively killing the mood.

"Yeah." Her voice lowered. I kicked myself for being so stupid. I tried to resurrect the call.

"I got your letter today."

"You did." Her voice bounced back to normal levels.

"I love your cartoons. They remind me of eighth grade art class." There was a pause and I could feel her smile through the phone.

"I remember drawing cartoon people with your sister. We sat at my parents' kitchen table for hours. After a while, I wanted to go watch TV or do something else, but Kelly just kept going and going until she got it perfect."

"That was her." There was pause as I think we both weren't sure if we were allowed to move the conversation on from the dead sister. Since the death was in my family, I determined it was my responsibility to resume.

"Well, I was really happy to get your letter. Made my day."

"I'm glad."

"As for Thanksgiving, I hadn't given it too much thought until just now. But, yes, I'd love to get coffee while I'm home."

"Great. How about Local Bean on Friday?"

"Sounds good. Will you be at your parents' place all weekend?"

"Yes. I'm driving up Wednesday to spend Thanksgiving with Mom, Dad, and Melissa. And then Glen, my boyfriend, will fly in on Saturday."

"Oh…"

"Maybe if you're still around we could all get together. I've told Glen all about you.

"Sure."

"Okay. See you Friday."

I hung up the phone and wondered what Allie told Glen about James Nakamura. *Did you tell him that you had to cheer me up in seventh grade after I didn't make the baseball team? Did you tell him how I was so jealous of your relationship with my little sister that I basically didn't talk to you for a year? Or perhaps how even though I didn't get your odd affinity for rabbits, I was the one who found Patches frozen stiff as a board and helped you bury him in your backyard despite the ground being frozen rock hard? Regardless, of course Allie Lockwood has a boyfriend. I'm sure there is no shortage of guys in Boston who love creative artist types.*

Even though I just learned about this Glen character, his existence didn't deter me from looking forward to seeing Allie. I wrote "Coffee w/ Allie" on the fourth Friday of November on my wall calendar and circled it twice. Staring at her name brought forth a flood of memories—a catalog of our greatest hits concluding with seeing her at the funeral a few weeks ago. My weekend game of blocking out terrible thoughts got much more competitive. I still wasn't winning, but Allie's letter gave me a fighting chance. And when the darkest thoughts came, they were softened by a recent memory: seeing my childhood crush again in the middle of that church gymnasium.

CHAPTER 4

SEMI-RHYTHMIC MOVEMENT

Allie's letter brought me back to the night of Kelly's funeral. My mom had recently sent me a video recording of the service the church produced, but I've never been able to watch it.

There's heaviness to that memory, which makes it too difficult to pop a tape into a VCR and relieve it. At the same time, amidst the pain and trauma, there were moments the camera didn't capture: small gestures of care and compassion that I will never forget.

The oversized coin felt heavier than expected when I retrieved it out of my coat pocket. With my right thumb, I pressed the metal disc into my left palm until it branded me, attempting to use physical pain to distract me from…well, everything else. The day before, Matthew Dunbar, a high school classmate, had presented me with his most valuable possession—a one-year sobriety chip from AA—as a security blanket. Things had not always gone easy in life for

Matthew, yet when I was drowning, he offered me his life preserver, putting my well-being ahead of his own.

I drove to the funeral alone because I needed a minute to myself. Sure, the dead sister support system was populous, well-intentioned, and overly eager to help, but it was also overwhelming. So much had been thrown at me the past few days, the twenty-minute solo ride allowed me to empty out part of my overcrowded mind. Carefully resting the coin in my coat pocket, I joined the rest of my family inside the church.

The vestry behind the sanctuary was an oblong room with robes of different sizes hung along one wall. Harsh overhead lighting illuminated the room, but did little to warm the space. Communion glasses were stored in stacked wooden holders on top of a worn out counter housing a sink. Next to the counter were three gold candle lighters with wood handles. Tonight's acolyte, a scrawny kid of twelve or thirteen swimming in his white robe, was selecting his candle lighter for the evening. More than likely, he was there knocking out confirmation requirements, the one on Pastor Gibson's list who was available on short notice. After the service, this kid would take off his oversized robe, catch a ride home, and not give Kelly Nakamura another thought. His sister was probably still alive.

Surveying the faces of my parents and my older sister, my body reconnected to the combination of nausea and heartbreak that had become normal. Over the past few days, I'd become accustomed to the solemn, sorrowful expressions we were wearing, like mirrors of each other's grief. Right before we headed out to take our seats, Pastor Gibson called us together. Perhaps this was the moment we might receive some spiritual guidance or some particularly insightful words of wisdom. We formed a sad huddle around the gray haired, middle-aged man as he secured his rope belt in place and paused before speaking.

"As soon as the service ends, everyone will follow you down to the gymnasium for the reception. Once you're in the gym, it's very important for the four of you to split up. Everyone will want to talk to you, and if you stay together, it will create a long receiving line. By scattering throughout the gym, the people who want to talk to you individually will be able to find you and talk to you."

My family was too tired and too emotionally numb to do anything but nod in the affirmative to the pastor's directive. The way we were gathered around him, with him giving us tactical guidance, it felt like he was the coach giving us a play during a time out. *This is the big one! We're just about to start the funeral for my little sister, who was all of twenty years old. Okay, guys—the most important thing right now and what we need to focus on is spacing on the court. Got it, coach!*

As soon as I heard the strains of my mom's favorite hymn, which signified the end of the service, I got up and briskly walked down the corridor to the reception. (We were also coached to get to our individual spots quickly.) As directed, I found my own space at the top of the key in order to keep the lane open.

The gym was spacious enough to house a couple hundred people comfortably. The wooden pull-out bleachers were stored in their upright positions and basketball backboards were raised to the top of the ceiling. Instead of a traditional basketball hardwood, the floor was covered in some sort of synthetic surface, probably a cost-cutting strategy. On the opposite wall across from the bleachers was a sliding window, which connected to the kitchen. Over the window, someone had crudely taped a homemade poster advertising the next youth group meeting.

Turns out Pastor Gibson knew his stuff and was not wrong to give his pregame advice. Within minutes, a steady stream of funeral attendees flowed out of the opening on the far side of the gymnasium, practically filling it to capacity. Once in the gym, they flocked to whichever member of the family they were most connected to. My mom was by far the biggest attraction; at one point, I couldn't see her through the throngs of friends encircling her. It was like media day before the Super Bowl, and she was the star of the team who attracted the most reporters hoping to get a quote or a sound bite. I had to admit, it would have been inefficient to have all people waiting in the same line for the four of us.

Just trying to survive this experience, I had given zero thought to who the guests at my sister's funeral would be or who I would have to talk to. Today's to-do list was finding a coat and tie, keeping my mom away from editing the pre-service playlist, and keeping emotional breakdowns to a minimum. But like any party, what makes for a great funeral are the guests you don't know or didn't expect to show up. Based on the last few days at my mom's house, I could have predicted the extended family and close friends that would be in attendance. However, there were people from my past—people who had followed the story of the missing young girl—and chose to show up for me at the absolute worst time in my life. For their surprising presence, I was truly grateful.

One of my high school friends, Joel Rappaport, had no business being there that evening. Not because we weren't close—we were—but he lived in Atlanta and had a law school exam the day before. Apparently, after acing his intellectual property test, he'd hopped in his car and driven overnight just to be there. Joel's presence, like Matthew's sobriety chip, was one of those small miracles of humanity that made this time just a bit more bearable.

Joel's parents, who watched us grow up on Little League diamonds and in carefully posed prom pictures, were in attendance as well. His father, Dr. Rappaport, was one the most respected law professors at Syracuse University, and he certainly looked the part in a gray tweed jacket and scholarly glasses. I don't think Dr. Rappaport said a word while his wife hugged me and filled the air with all the traditional funeral lines. But it was his expression I will always remember. With serious eyes and pierced lips, he communicated a well of feelings for me, the vastness of which I had no idea ran so deep. Previously, I assumed he thought I was just Joel's goofy friend, but now, I felt so seen and loved by a man I respected so much as a man and as a father. I never heard Dr. Rappaport say anything on this night; his silence spoke volumes. A brilliant legal mind, he seemed to know that at this moment, no argument or words could bring comfort. So, he consoled me in silence.

My high school English teacher was not as efficient with her words. After hugging me, she completely lost her usual eloquence, which made her a wonderful and beloved AP Literature teacher. "This is bad. This is really, really, really bad," she announced and empathetically gestured outwardly with her arms for emphasis. Mrs.

Barron wrote one of my letters of recommendation for college, and I can only hope she displayed a greater range of vocabulary when she pitched my better qualities to admission offices. That being said, her histrionic response to a horrible situation was honest and unfiltered, kind of like my students' cards.

The parade of mourners was non-stop. As soon as one conversation ended, another one began with someone wanting to share their version of "she's now in a better place." After what seemed like hours, finally my crowd dissipated and I had a chance to catch my breath.

That's when I saw the ultimate surprise guest, Allie Lockwood. It had been eight years since we graduated from high school and more than that since we had really been friends, but there she was. Standing on the sidelines, just past half-court, her legs crossed behind a long dark patterned skirt. She had just finished a conversation and looked my way when our eyes met. She looked great. Her girlish face had matured, but she still had those innocent blue eyes and soft blonde hair. She was taller and thinner than I remembered, and I certainly didn't recall black sweaters fitting her quite so well. For a split second in time, just like in the movies, I couldn't hear or see anyone or anything else; it was just Allie and I standing alone on a church gymnasium floor. We closed the distance between us and shared a hug.

"James, I am so sorry." I heard the same words so many times, but when Allie said it, it felt personalized and genuine.

"Thanks." And then we stood there and looked at each other's feet for a while. She was wearing black shoe boots that were scuffed on the toes.

"What you said up there was beautiful. Probably helped a lot of people."

"Do you think so?"

"Yes I do." And again, her short response rang with more truth and resonance than anyone else had said over the past few days. I couldn't believe she was here now. Even though we hadn't talked in years, it felt like we had been linked together since alphabetic order placed our desks next to each other at the start of middle school. This was the girl who asked me to the eighth grade dance and then sprained her ankle at soccer practice, depriving me of any slow dances with wandering hands. There I was, talking to the same Allie Lockwood who'd been both a friend and an artistic mentor to my younger sister. Regrettably, her friendship with Kelly blossomed shortly after she had rejected my sophomore year offer of "more than friends," which led to some uncomfortable times. I hadn't thought about Allie in years, but there was no one I'd rather be talking to right at this instant. In a weird and bizarre way, I couldn't escape the feeling that being with her felt like home.

"Well, I was just trying to get through it," to which she nodded and then I continued. "So what are you up to? Are you still around here?"

"No, I'm in Boston. I went to art school there and decided to stay. I'm actually trying to make it as a painter."

"That's so cool. You are ridiculously talented." Allie walked me through the mechanics of how paintings by living artists were monetized and the struggle to have one critic find your work interesting.

I explained to her the glamor and prestige that was teaching first grade in suburban New Jersey.

"I bet your students must love you."

"I don't mean to brag, but I'm kind of a big deal." I replied sarcastically. To which, Allie smiled that smile—that same smile she'd been giving me for years that said, "You're funny, but not quite as funny as you think you are." She gave me that look back in sixth grade when I would flip through our outdated science text and make up alternative captions for the pictures, usually involving our homeroom teacher's love life. For some reason, my overestimation of my sense of humor made her happy, which in turn, made me smile.

My wounded heart slowly began to beat with a newfound rhythm, and I didn't want our conversation to end. As we ran out of the usual topics, I glanced around the gym, searching for anything to talk about. The packed space had emptied out, leaving only Allie and me, and a custodian lurking in the corner waiting to lock up. Even without words, I sensed a gravitational pull toward her. Allie's black boot tapped the synthetic floor surface, and I shifted my weight back and forth trying to think of something to say. Even though this semi-rhythmic movement in a gym didn't happen back at our middle school, perhaps it was the slow dance we were supposed to have so many years ago.

We shared contact info and vowed to stay in touch. Streams of light cut through the dark parking lot as Allie and I found our cars. An extended sigh of relief left my lungs as I loosened my tie and reclined in my front seat. I reached for Matthew's sobriety chip, holding it up to examine it closer. The letters in the word "Recovery" reflected back at me, and for a brief moment, I wondered if that was something within reach. The metal token made a pleasing "thunk" as I dropped it in my cup holder and turned over the ignition. As far as I knew, they didn't give out chips for dead sisters, but I was only four days into my non-existent twelve-step program. I was sure when I got to the one-year mark I'd be all but cured.

CHAPTER 5

THE YOUNGEST OLD PERSON

A week before my coffee with Allie, I was sitting in my classroom, staring out the window, when Linda Gale popped through my door. She taught fifth grade and was the kind of teacher who would open up her Christmas "teacher" gifts in front of her whole class even though there would be one or two kids who hadn't gotten her anything. Still, the district loved her, and if Greenridge's middle-aged ladies had a head-cheerleader, it would probably be Linda. Without any greeting, she launched into her agenda.

"Are you going out to lunch?"

"No, not today." Ever since returning, I had not joined the Friday lunch crew.

"Then can I ask you a favor?"

"I guess." I immediately regretted my answer, having no idea what would come next.

"Shannon just had a pretty rough observation." Shannon was Linda's student teacher from Rutgers. Her supervising professor must have come to observe her teach a lesson and write up a formal evaluation. I looked at Linda directly waiting for what came next. "Well… she's pretty upset about it." And then she shrugged her shoulders with what I thought was shocking deference. "Anyway, I'm heading out to lunch. Would you mind talking to her and seeing if she's okay?"

Without waiting for an answer, Linda turned and called out to someone walking down the hall for a ride to Roberto's. Lunch was a pretty big deal at Greenridge. It was a necessary break from teaching vowel patterns or discussing the Revolutionary War. When you spend your entire day surrounded by elementary-aged children, the chance for an adult conversation is a crucial mental recharge. On Fridays, many of the teachers would go out to lunch, which was the social highlight of the week. Since Linda Gale didn't want to miss her weekly Cobb Salad and gossip session, emotional support was a task that apparently could be delegated. *After all, empathy and compassion aren't exactly prerequisites for being head cheerleader.*

Truth be told, I was the logical person for Linda to ask for help. We had recently become a "teaching" school, hosting three to four student teachers each semester. All of our interns were twenty to twenty-five years behind the typical Greenridge teacher: marriage, kids, and minivans were quite some time off. Only a few years out of college myself, I was approachable and someone they could talk to. I was like a high school pitcher visiting a Little League practice coached by middle-aged men; the kids always know who the "youngest old person" is and gravitate to them. With a fair knowledge of college radio and a short educational resume, I became the patron saint of Greenridge student teachers.

But what the actual fuck, Linda Gale? A graduate student you've been mentoring for the past two months falls on her face and you're not going to be there to help her pick up the pieces? Have a great lunch!

The wing for the upper grades was on the other side of the building. Upon entering Linda's classroom I could see Dawn and Megan, the two other student teachers that semester, were already there doing their best to revive the patient.

Shannon was hunched over a chair with a tissue in hand. Her natural Irish complexion had been colored red with tears and emotion, her long, curly hair tightly pulled back into a bun secured with a shiny black barrette. For a student teacher, she was impeccably dressed—a professional black skirt, white blouse, and tights. Her large olive eyes met mine as I entered the room without a flicker of expression. If it had been another Greenridge veteran checking on her, she probably would have tried to put on a braver face. She was mid-explanation, recounting what had happened.

"He said my classroom management was so subpar...he said the students were actually trying to make up for my lack of structure and clear expectations...that I put the students in a place of having to perform instead of putting the priority on learning." I had never seen this girl teach, but the criticism sounded like garbage to me. "He said there was no closing...the lesson just ended with the bell ringing."

"I heard he does that with every first observation," Dawn chimed in. "That he never gives positive feedback until his last trip."

Megan gently rubbed Shannon's back and made a sad face toward Dawn and me, empathizing with what she was going through. I didn't really know what to say; I wanted to ask what Linda had said, but obviously Shannon's cooperating teacher was useless today.

"So...you'll get another chance?" was my attempt to be forward thinking.

"He comes back in two weeks," Shannon murmured between drying her eyes.

"If you want, I can get some sixth-graders to beat him up at the bike racks?" It wasn't the best joke, but I was glad to see Shannon crack a hint of smile. The four of us talked through all of lunch and recess, and Shannon eventually got herself composed enough to get through the rest of the day. The four of us agreed to go out for a drink after school to continue commiserating and celebrate the end of the week. About five minutes before the bell, Linda strolled in and looked at our support group condescendingly like we were intruding on her territory. She threw down her purse and met eyes with Shannon.

"All better?" she asked, like she just put a Band-Aid on the knee of a toddler.

Jesus Christ.

I'm sure the girls were more used to college bars in New Brunswick with their cheap pitchers, bright lights, and loud popular music. But Finley's was the best bar we had in Ashford Park. Well, it was the only bar we had in Ashford Park. From the outside, it looked like a nondescript white house with black shutters. The inside was filled with dark wood, cigarette smoke, and seventies guitar rock.

The interior design was a mix of nautical and wild west, with a splash of Irish pub thrown in for good measure. It was unclear if the focal point was intended to be the battered Golden Tee video game on the back wall or the giant inflatable penguin perched above the bar. Finley's had no fruity cocktails with names that served as sexual double entendre; it was "a beer and a shot" kind of place. So the three Rutgers students, probably the best looking Finley's patrons in quite some time, were drinking bottles of light beer at a high-top table when I arrived.

"It kind of feels like they want to criticize you no matter what you do." Apparently, we were still on the bashing of supervising professors. Megan continued, "I feel like I'll do exactly what I was told to do, and then they'll tell me to do the exact opposite. One week, I was told I talked too much, so the students weren't active enough. Then the next week, the students were confused because I didn't give enough direction."

"Sometimes, it does feel like a no-win situation," Dawn noted with resolve.

"And if Professor Willis knows so much about literacy, why isn't he teaching second grade?" Megan asked. We all laughed, noting the hypocrisy of trying to learn education from professors who weren't very good at teaching.

"It's like a personal trainer who is out-of-shape," I offered.

"Or my high school guidance counselor," Dawn suggested. "Who was Mrs. Gulden to offer any kind of advice on being successful? She was a sad, divorced lady whose office walls were covered with weird motivational posters from the sixties."

To this point, Shannon had been rather quiet, and it was evident she was still somewhat bothered by the day's events. Yet, the support of her peers and 4.2% alcohol by volume was starting to turn the tide. By the second beer, she worked her way into the conversation.

"Hey…I'm sorry about today. I didn't mean to make it all about me." Silence gripped the table as we tried to make sense of this unnecessary apology. Megan shot her a confused stare from across the table.

"What are you talking about? You had a crappy day. You don't have to apologize."

"I guess. I feel bad that you guys had to manage me."

"Oh please," Dawn said as Megan leaned over and gave Shannon a half-hearted hug without getting out of her seat. Shannon received the affection with an awkward smile.

The conversation moved on to parties, job opportunities, and the prospect of moving back in with your parents. After a drink, Megan and Dawn left as they headed together to the same sorority party. Shannon and I decided to stay and get something to eat; apparently crying through lunch had not provided much nourishment. We handed menus back to a waitress and found ourselves making somewhat uncomfortable eye contact.

"Can I ask you a question?"

"Sure."

"Earlier when you apologized about making it about you—what was that about?" Shannon immediately retreated behind crossed arms and a confused look. In response, I tried to retract my question, "You don't have to talk about it if you don't want to."

"No, it's okay. I guess….it comes from being one of nine kids. Growing up, we had to be really independent, take care of ourselves. My parents didn't have a lot of attention to spread around, so when one of us cried, threw a tantrum in the grocery store, my parents… my dad…would…get angry." The word "angry" seemed loaded with hurt and bad memories.

"I'm sorry. I didn't mean to pry."

"It's okay." Shannon paused, trying to make conversation. "What about you? How many brothers and sist—?" And before she could even finish the sentence Shannon was struck with the realization that she was student teaching at a school with a teacher whose sister recently killed herself. She exhaled deeply and apologized, "James, I am so sorry. I wasn't thinking, I didn't mean…"

"Please; it's totally okay," I reassured her. But, it wasn't okay. Shannon's innocuous question poked my fresh wound and reminded me once again of the wealth of pain I had access to at a moment's notice.

Eventually, we found topics to discuss that weren't angry fathers or dead sisters: music, food, life right after college.

"You didn't drink coffee in college?"

"Not a drop."

"And you drink it black, like an old man?" The corners of her mouth turned upward, and there were flecks of light in her olive eyes when she smiled.

"Well, my first coffee mentor taught me that coffee is supposed to be bitter and that you shouldn't add sugar because it antagonizes the bean."

"Coffee mentor? Antagonizes the bean? Who talks like that?" She had a lively, expressive quality to her voice, which was endearing. "No, thank you. Lots of cream and four sugars for me."

"So, basically if I took coffee ice cream, allowed it to melt, and reheated it in a mug, that would be your ideal coffee shop order?"

"That sounds delicious." As she spoke, I couldn't take my eyes off the curvature of her lips, their perfection only disrupted by a vertical scar on her bottom lip. I wanted to ask her how she got it, but after accidentally uncovering the grocery store trauma, I was hesitant. Shannon later revealed to me that, as a little girl, she cut her lip on a thorn when she was smelling a rose—hurt by trying to get too close to something so beautiful.

After sharing a couple appetizers, we found ourselves in another unfamiliar silence. I spoke next.

"Got any plans for the weekend?

"We're going to the football game tomorrow morning. I'm going to the airport to pick up my boyfriend."

Of course.

CHAPTER 6

THE BRIDGE

Local Bean was a pretty trendy coffee shop for my remarkably unhip hometown. It recently took up residence in one half of a brick building on Main Street, refreshing a space previously occupied by a now defunct travel agency. The building was shared with Esposito's, our favorite high school pizza place and popular after school hang out. I spotted a couple of bookish-looking teenage girls by the window and supposed the more sophisticated high school crowd now strolled into the coffee shop for a latte, a mocha, or perhaps even a melted, reheated coffee ice cream.

I arrived well before our appointed meeting time and was greeted by the hissing of milk steamers and the maudlin strains of some acoustic singer/songwriter playing through the stereo. The earthy, rich aroma of roasting beans filled the room, and I was looking forward to a real cup of coffee. Just as I was about to get in line, I was gripped with panic on how to proceed in this social situation.

Should I get coffee or wait for her before ordering? If I wait, should I offer to pay? Am I here too early? Should I go back outside and pretend I'm just arriving? I should have brought a book that I could be reading and casually look up from when she walks in.

Ultimately, I decided on waiting to order coffee and sat down at a table in the corner. I fidgeted in my seat and looked conspicuously around the room. I rubbed my sweaty palms against my jeans as I tried to slow my breathing. *Geez! What was I so nervous about? This was her idea.* A gentleman at the next table left, and I grabbed his abandoned copy of *The Times*. For the next few minutes, I stared at the shape and formation of the black words on the white page, but I couldn't possibly actually make sense of the story about the communist satellite state and who was or wasn't sending military or financial aid. Come to think of it, this article might have been about fashion week or a quarterback controversy; I couldn't possibly think about anything else besides the girl I was about to have coffee with.

"Hey there!" Suddenly, she was standing right in front of me: blue jeans, cream-colored turtleneck sweater, and camel jacket. I got up and gave her a hug inhaling the smell of her shampoo. Creepy—yes, but she still smelled good. I froze awkwardly until she spoke again.

"Should we get something to drink?'

"Yes."

I ordered a black coffee and Allie asked for the herbal tea selection. A heavily bearded barista ran down a bunch of hippie-inspired green teas: Allie selected one and turned to me with a broad smile.

"Since I invited you, I would like to pay," she proudly announced.

"Why, thank you," I replied and then without thinking added the unnecessary observation, "This day just keeps getting better all the time!" I must have been nervous. *"This day just keeps getting better all the time?!" What a dork! You better up your game because cheeseball lines like that are not going to get it done.*

Allie retrieved her wallet out of purse and a bright green sticky note fell to the floor. I promptly picked it up and offered it back to Allie, noticing it was covered with a series of numbers.

"Here you go."

"Thanks! Those are Glen's sizes," as if I was supposed to know what that meant.

"Glen's sizes?"

"Yes, sizes for clothes. If I'm out shopping, and I want to get him a shirt or something, I like to have his sizes handy." Allie extended the sticky note so I could confirm that Glen wore 35" sleeve in dress shirts. I pictured him as a sizable gentleman—maybe not as tall as Laundry Cart Girl's boyfriend—but likely bigger than me.

"You said he's flying in this weekend?"

"No, he's not going to make it. It's a long story." Allie broke eye contact and made it clear it was a long story she was not interested in telling at this time. Based on the evidence on hand, I tried to do an on-the-fly forensic study of this relationship: Allie is committed enough to keeping clothes sizes on hand, but perhaps there's some dispute on why he's not visiting the family after Thanksgiving? I would have to gather more clues.

"What does Glen do?"

"He's in graduate school getting a PhD in computer science," Allie replied very matter-of-factly. *Hmmm...she seems bored by that.* Seeing as though I took one computer science class in college and remembered almost nothing, I abandoned any further questions about the man's profession.

We got our drinks and sat back down. For a while, we spoke about the mundane aspects of our lives: rent, pop culture, who we've stayed in touch with from high school, etc. While I had maintained a handful of meaningful relationships, Allie had made a "clean break" from high school and only came home to see her mom and dad. She inquired about my family.

"So your mom's remarried?"

"No, but she's been living with someone for a year and half. Seems pretty committed."

"And your dad?"

"There seem to be a few suitors circling Mr. Nakamura." Allie giggled and put her hands around her mug of Hibiscus Haze as if to warm them. *Man, was she attractive.* She was cute in high school, but now she was stone-cold beautiful.

"Until last month, I didn't know your parents got divorced."

"Yeah, they got separated pretty much right after graduation. Divorce was final a few years later."

"Do you...do you think that the divorce had anything to do...?" I took in Allie's question and for a second thought about my younger sister growing up in a less happy house than the one I did. On some level it's rude to have someone ask why your sister killed herself, but I think Allie was genuinely curious. I also had to allow for the fact that I didn't have a monopoly on grief. Allie was experiencing loss too and searching for answers.

"I do." I looked directly at Allie in the eyes as I slowly nodded my head up and down. Allie took her right hand off her mug and placed it on top of my left hand. I could feel the residual heat from her mug and her figurative warmth as well. Her hand was soft and delicate, and I never wanted her to move it.

"James, it must be so hard." Those words coming from someone else would have sounded trite, but out of the mouth of Allie Lockwood, they came off as earnest and genuine.

"I don't think that's the only reason, but I do think my older sister, Jackie, and I got a happier version of my parents' marriage for a longer stretch of time." Allie took her other hand and put it in my left hand. We sat there for a while looking at each other and holding hands. As much as I wanted this contact, I was a little conflicted because now I didn't have a free hand to drink my coffee with. *But what was this subtle hand-on-hand action? Was this one friend consoling another? Was this me on my way to getting my own sticky note with dress shirt sizes?*

Eventually, we unclasped hands and I was able to finish my coffee. It was no longer at the ideal drinking temperature, but it was vastly superior to the Mr. Percolator swill I had been having at my mom's. It didn't matter; the temperature, taste, or the quality of the coffee was immaterial at this time. I was with Allie Lockwood, and there was no one on this planet I would rather be with. I looked at the bottom of my cup, and I wanted our time together to continue.

"Do you want to walk to the Falls?"

"Sure."

"The Falls" was local slang to describe where Main Street crossed the Cayuga River. It really wasn't a river (more of a stream) and it absolutely wasn't a waterfall (just a gentle descent over some rocks). In addition to the road traversing the "river," there was a pedestrian bridge that led to a small park. It was a truss style bridge built years ago and pictured prominently on anything featuring the town's name. It was popular with both little boys throwing rocks and engaged couples taking announcement photos.

We walked to the middle of the bridge and leaned over the railing. We were facing the wider part of the river before it hit the rocks downstream. For old time's sake, I picked up a small stone off the bridge and hurled it as far as I could; it made a little "blip" in the water. I looked over at Allie who seemed unimpressed by my imaginary relay throw into the infield. She was staring at the water deep in a memory.

"What are you thinking about?"

"Kelly."

"Oh...what in particular?"

"The time we walked down here from my house because...because of donuts."

"Donuts...that would have taken you like forty minutes to walk here from your house!"

"I know. We were in my living room and just started talking about jelly doughnuts and how the jelly inside jelly donuts really doesn't taste like regular jelly. And then, we decided we needed to conduct a taste test of powdered sugar vs. glazed jelly donuts. So, we bought some at Calvins and ate them on that bench right over there." Allie pointed at a bench in the park under a tree.

When she turned her head back to the river, the wind blew her hair in front of her face and she used her hand to tame it behind her right ear. Everything about her face was perfect and right at this moment, I couldn't stop studying the line where her cheek met her neck.

I was staring at her, and she could feel me staring at her. I knew what I wanted, and she knew it as well. For a moment, she looked at the water as if the answer was out there. In slow motion, she finally turned to me and her light blue eyes said "yes" without speaking a word. We leaned into each other, and our lips met halfway across the bridge. It wasn't long, but it was magical enough to make the rest of the world vanish. The kiss, fifteen years in the making, was both infused with familiar memories and brimming with the promise of something new. For someone who spent a great deal of life worrying about the past or agonizing about the future—like whether to order coffee while waiting to meet someone—this was a rare moment of pure action unburdened by thought.

After a kiss of undeniable length and intensity, one that could never be mistaken as consolatory, Allie smiled and gave me that familiar look.

"Just to be clear-this is not what I had in mind when I invited you to coffee."

"I sure am glad you sent me that letter."

We laughed and hugged before walking back toward town hand in hand.

This day just keeps getting better all the time.

CHAPTER 7

TESTING THE WATERS

I floated through the next two days, spending as much time with Allie as I could. Every time I left the house, my mom asked if I was "going to see that cute girl from middle school," which I think made her happy because I had someone to talk to. My mom was big on talking about feelings and blamed my father's inability to do so for a lot of their marital problems. I think she assumed I was running off to Allie so she could play therapist and help me process my grief. Maybe that's what was going on, but I just wanted to kiss her again.

More than the prospect of another make-out session, being with Allie was a refuge, a safe haven, shielding me from the misery in my life. Things didn't hurt so badly when I was with her. Even when Allie brought up Kelly, it wasn't painful; somehow, it was blissfully nostalgic when she shared memories.

In addition to the doses of emotional novocaine, there was also the tantalizing prospect that our lips might find each other again.

There's unpredictability and excitement in having a new kissing partner. Sometimes walking by her side, my distracted mind would be thinking *just because it happened once doesn't mean it will happen again.* And then when it did, I'd gleefully remember, *Oh yeah, we do this now.* Only she and I had membership to this hidden world where our kisses were our secrets.

Allie and I both knew each other's parents, who would have warmly welcomed us for dinner. Alternatively, we could have tracked down a high school classmate for a drink, but we knew instinctively that this time was just for us. The protective bubble around us only had room for two. Christmas season had just begun, and the town was being adorned with the usual decorations: banners on the light posts, white lights strung across Main Street, images of Santa painted on storefront windows. Allie and I walked all over town, sometimes deep in conversation, sometimes saying nothing.

Allie listened to me with a curious and sympathetic ear, judiciously asking questions about how I was doing with carefully selected words. In high school, she was that quiet girl who seemed wise beyond her years, never wasting time on pointless chatter. Now, I could almost see the ideas swirl around her brain as she nodded, acknowledging my responses. I appreciated that she didn't always feel the need to fill the silence, sometimes letting ideas—no matter how painful or uncomfortable—linger in the air, giving them room to be fully considered. After a healthy session of walking and conversation, Allie's nose was red from the chill of November, so we took shelter in The Village Tavern.

Over glasses of red wine at the bar, Allie offered to show me some of her work in progress. From her purse, she unearthed a small sketchbook, which was filled with thoughts, ideas, and rough drafts of future pieces. I flipped through the pages, and somehow it made sense that these complex and abstract visual ideas came from the same girl who doodled flowers and hearts in Mr. Hannigan's social studies class. Even though nothing was a finished project, her ideas were incredibly impressive: accessible yet progressive, somehow challenging and comforting at the same time. Well, that's at least what I would have said on National Public Radio if I were an art critic. The most complete sketch featured a nondescript figure surrounded by a swirling spiral pattern.

"Is this meant to be the ocean? A wave?"

"It could be," Allie said coyly. I examined the figure closely. It definitely was meant to be a human and even without any facial details, it seemed to evoke something…maybe fear…anger?

"The wave is engulfing the person?"

"That's what you think is happening?" *Hmm…maybe I am in therapy.* On second look, the wave could have been an extension of the figure or manifestation of the figure's thoughts.

"Well, I like this one," as if I was some big time art investor, "I'd love to see it finished."

"You're very kind," Allie rolled her eyes.

We had an "art is ambiguous" conversation, and I drew upon my college skills—both as a philosophy major and as a late night drunk debater—to hold my own. Allie was smart, maybe too smart for me, but she let me into her world and never exposed any of my cultural illiteracy.

Our leisurely afternoon continued with some Christmas shopping for Allie's nephews. Walking through the aisles of a toy shop, we bantered back and forth, opining that toys weren't nearly as good as they used to be. An old woman paying for a jigsaw puzzle was visibly amused at our antics. She didn't say "Oh, what a cute couple" out loud, but her endearing look certainly communicated that she was thinking exactly that. This was my time with Allie—shopping in a boutique toy store with a beautiful girl while the world smiled upon us. It was a wonderful place to be and I wanted to stay there forever.

Of course, shopping for gifts in Tiny Treasures couldn't last forever. The demands of teaching first grade were calling, and Allie presumably had a picture of a man surrounded by a wave to finish painting. Before Allie's flight we agreed to meet on Sunday—of all places in the parking lot of our old middle school. Nostalgic setting aside, it was roughly halfway between our parents' houses and sat next to a park.

The path to the pond was familiar, worn smooth by countless steps taken in our youth. In seventh grade, Mr. Levinson would have us collect water samples to examine under a microscope. I don't recall which single-cell organisms we were supposed to be looking for, but we loved having class outside. In the winter, the water froze over, and "Hamburger Pond" was a popular ice-skating destination, where we'd glide laps around the burger-shaped island that inspired its nickname. But today, I wasn't hunting paramecium or playing pickup hockey; as I stared at the pond, I wondered where we'd be when the water froze solid.

"So, what are you doing for Christmas?"

"James." Just by the way she uttered my name I could tell I shouldn't have asked. Allie and I had been living in the present, and my question just brought up the prospect of the future. In a few hours, I'd be in a car and she'd be on a plane, perhaps both of us considering the ramifications of our actions this weekend. The difference was she was in a relationship and I was not. To this point, I hadn't worried about what the kisses meant, but it seemed Allie was doing just that.

"Do you want to know why Glen didn't come this weekend?"

"I suppose," I replied indifferently even though I was quite interested in the answer.

"Last week he and I got in a huge fight, and you know what it was about?"

"No." Suspense building.

"You."

"Me?"

"Ever since Kelly died, Glen says all I talk about is you. That... that it's obvious...that I have feelings for you. And...based on the last two days...I'd say he's right." Allie Lockwood admitting she had feelings for me should have been a glorious feeling, but her resigned and conflicted look made the mood a little less celebratory. Allie was in a delicate place and instead of treading lightly, like an idiot, I told her how I felt.

"Allie, I adore you." This made the conflict on Allie's face even worse as she shook her head, and she wiped away a tear from her eye. "James…don't…" She was lost.

"Well, maybe we don't have to figure this out right now. This weekend has been amazing. I'd really like to see you again. Would you like to see me again?"

Allie did the thing where she slowly nodded, letting the idea marinate. After a moment, she looked at me, agreeing with her eyes. "Yes, I would."

Allie wiped her eyes again, and we hugged, freezing time until a bird squealed from a tree above. Holding hands as we walked back toward the school, I imagined telling my seventh-grade self, gripping that plastic bag of pond water, that it all worked out—we got the girl! We embraced until the prospect of missing her flight became a reality; Allie gave me a smile and a wave as she drove off. I exhaled and took a look at the trees and the sky. Kicking the gravel of the parking lot made a sound that interrupted the quiet morning. Once again, I was alone.

By the time I got on the Thruway, I was deep in over-analysis and rethinking my message to my seventh-grade self. *So you're falling for this girl who has a boyfriend. How much risk does this Glen present? He's like a computer science guy. Over time, Allie is going to choose me. Then, we'll move back home, get married, and have kids. I could get a job at Westfield Elementary, probably become the principal someday. Second graders would bring me a cupcake on their birthdays, and I'd reach into my desk and give them a special fancy pencil. No doubt about it; over time, Allie is going to pick me. I just have to hang in there.*

CHAPTER 8

YANKEE SWAP

The holidays are a pretty frenetic time in elementary school, and my giddy first graders were caught up in all of it. The prospect of Santa as well as the first snowfall made memorizing new sight words much harder than usual. I was distracted too, not by a man in a red suit from the North Pole, but by a blonde girl in ripped jeans from Boston. With everyone's minds elsewhere, it was not our best stretch of teaching and learning in Room 22.

Allie and I spoke on the phone a couple times, and as much as I loved hearing her voice, it was a poor substitute for being with her in person. The protective cocoon that previously enveloped around us couldn't span the distance. Allie couldn't be there in person after school, on the weekends, or shopping for milk, so Grief was there, more than happy to keep me company. In addition to the distance, I was filled with this sense that our whirlwind Thanksgiving weekend was just a dream. *Was Allie still thinking about kissing at The Falls or was she now grounded back in reality of painting and her computer science boyfriend? When would Allie and I have the time and space to make another connection?* Sitting at the dining table, phone receiver pressed to my face, I tried to keep these thoughts out of my brain and stay present with Allie.

Truth be told, thinking about Allie and Glen was better than thinking about my dead sister. Those waves of pain still had low and high tides; typically, the end of the school day was when I was awash with anxiety and sorrow. I delayed my commute home as long as possible, staying at school two or three hours past the final bell. I looked for company wherever I could find it.

Sheri, one of the fourth grade teachers, was the closest thing I had to a peer on the faculty. Barely in her thirties, she was roughly my age, but her two kids and subsequent divorce had aged her significantly past her chronological years. On Tuesdays, her ex-husband had the kids, and Sheri stayed after school. I looked forward to Sheri's late day because she would let me come by her classroom, steal some candy from her class prize bin, and distract her from grading maps of the regions of New Jersey. That was my life: tracking my colleagues' custody schedules just to avoid another lonely evening.

One Tuesday, after Sheri had enough of my shenanigans, I started the lonely walk back to the primary wing. The halls were empty, and the sound of my pen against the metal stair railing reverberated into the cavernous space. I was going to cut across the gym, when I noticed there was light seeping underneath the door of the faculty room. Besides Sheri, I figured all the teachers would have left to pick up kids or to go Christmas shopping. Poking my head up to the glass pane in the door, I spotted Shannon standing over the photocopier. She nodded as I walked in, and I figured I should look like I had a reason to be there. I rustled through my pockets and came up with enough change for a raspberry iced tea. After a sip of Snapple, I used the fact under the cap as my opener.

"Did you know goldfish have a nine-second attention span?" I offered her.

"Longer than fifth-grade boys then?" She responded without missing a beat.

"What are you doing here so late?"

"Killing some trees so I can teach division of fractions." Shannon smiled as she pointed to her highly collated output with sets of practice problems.

"Where would any of us be today without knowing how to multiply by the reciprocal? Make sure to tell your class that when they grow up they'll have to divide by fractions all the time."

"All the time," Shannon repeated and stifled a laugh. "What about you? What are you doing here at this late hour?"

"You know…nothing better to do. Staying after school keeps me off the streets and out of trouble." By no means my best stuff. I took another sip and allowed the whirring and humming of the photocopier to fill the silence.

"Are you going to the Christmas party on Friday?" I asked.

"Err…I don't know. Wasn't planning on it. I don't think Dawn and Megan are going. Plus it's the opposite direction from my place. I'd have to drive home after school, change, and come back past here to get there."

"Well, that certainly sounds unadventurous for someone your age," I scolded her sarcastically. "Why don't you do this? After school on Friday, you can come back to my place. You can change there and then we'll head over together." The invitation felt bold, even presumptuous, and I wondered if I had hastily crossed a line. *Did I just make plans with Shannon outside of school?* I'm not quite sure why solving Shannon's transportation problems or her presence at the holiday party was so important to me, but all of sudden, I had turned into Mr. Problem Solver. Maybe I wanted someone my age to be there, so I wouldn't have to pretend to care about conversations about lazy husbands or easy dinners to make after school. Shannon seemed taken aback by my offer, tilting her head slightly to assess its audacity before responding.

"Sure, but we'd still have three hours to kill. What are we going to do?"

"We could go see a movie?"

As she considered the possibility, her eyes bounced back and forth like she was following an imaginary volley over a net. After a lengthy rally, she acquiesced, "Okay, I'm in. What's your address?"

We made the necessary travel arrangements, and I scanned the faculty room for a newspaper in an effort to find movie times.

The lone matinee that fit our schedule was the annual animated cash grab, complete with fast-food tie-ins and an avalanche of plastic toy merchandising. We ate popcorn in the practically vacant theater, following the predictable tale of Scout the border collie learning the real meaning of Christmas. Periodically, I stole glances of her face when it was briefly illuminated by the glowing light of the movie screen, her tight curls framing her features.

It was painfully obvious very early in the movie that Scout would give up his opportunity to be a police dog in order to spend Christmas with his family, and my mind and my eyes kept wandering toward the graduate student sitting to my right. When she started in the fall, I didn't notice how cute she was: bright eyes, smooth, clear complexion, and round curvy lips. *Was I interested? Should I be interested? I spent a great weekend with Allie, but she made clear that Glen was still in the picture. It may not matter anyway; Shannon mentioned she also has a boyfriend.* In the midst of my deliberations, Shannon shot me a feigned smile, which I think was her reaction to a pack of corgis going caroling. I leaned back my seat and watched as Scout was trying to determine if he should go back home. *Don't worry, buddy. You'll figure it out.*

As the credits began to roll over, the annual Greenridge Christmas party was already underway at the vice-principal's house. Jill Novak lived in the newer section of Ashford Park, outside of the original enclave of one story homes that sprang up in the 1960s. Our school was designed as a central point for the original development to allow families the opportunity to walk to school. As wealth moved into the area, bigger and gaudier houses sprung up on the outside of the original community. Jill lived in one of these developments called Henderson Acres.

My Nissan Sentra rolled up to the stone-walled neighborhood monument, and I dug the party invite out of my pocket. Retrieving and inputting the guest gate code Jill provided, two serious-looking black iron gates swung inward. The neighborhood was made up of wide streets and sizable yards. Each stately two-story house had a long driveway and sat back off the road. Roof lines were tastefully decorated with warm white lights that had been hung with precision and discipline.

"I think this might be the neighborhood that *A Holiday for Scout* was based on...," I mused.

"Look at these houses. You could fit two of my parent's houses inside one of these. Can you imagine owning a house like this someday?"

"I don't have to. I already do. That crappy one bedroom apartment you saw earlier? That's just my flop house. I only live there to be closer to school." We chuckled and continued to take in the impressive real estate around us. Sure enough, Jill's house was the most ornately decorated in a cul-de-sac at the top of the neighborhood. In addition to the lights on the house, three perfectly symmetrical evergreen trees were adorned with evenly spaced strings of lights and oversize ornaments. Two more Christmas trees flanked a double door entry that was surrounded by a brick facade.

The inside of Jill's home might have been even more impressive than the exterior. The high ceiling foyer opened to set up curved stairs with an ornate handrail illuminated by a glitzy chandelier. Mr. Novak obviously did something for a living which paid significantly better than being a public educator. As Shannon and I waded through a living room of middle-aged women in tacky sweaters and stretch pants, Sheri caught my eye as she was getting a drink. Sheri subtly shot me a raised eyebrow wordlessly asking "Are you two together?"

There was a note of disappointment on her face when I shook my head dismissively in return. Shannon went off to find Linda, and I took up a spot next to Sheri and the half empty bottles of merlot.

"Mr. Nakamura—bringing the student teacher to the Christmas party...."

"Knock it off." I rummaged through a tub of soft drinks and beers until I found a seasonal ale that seemed acceptable.

"She's cute," Sheri observed looking at Shannon from across the room.

"She's got a boyfriend."

"Aren't you with your high-school sweetheart?"

I let out a half laugh. "We weren't together in high school, and we're not exactly together now. She also has a boyfriend."

"You know, a woman saying she 'has a boyfriend' could mean any number of things. She could be saying it to distance herself or to make herself seem more desirable. Or perhaps she says she has a boyfriend to convince herself she actually does." Sheri was a couple of glasses of wine into the evening.

"Or she could actually have a boyfriend."

"That too." Sheri took a long sip from her wine glass.

"Do you ever tell a guy you have a boyfriend?"

"Absolutely not. When you're a divorced mother of two, having a boyfriend—real or imaginary—isn't really a factor. Any guy vaguely interested in me doesn't care about that; he's trying to figure out how honest he can be with himself about taking on my truckload of emotional baggage."

Only a few sips into my beer, I wasn't ready for this level of realism. As I tried to think of something to say, Sheri shot me with the "I'm older than you and I've lived it, so I know it's true" look. Before I could respond, Sheri was summoned by the art teacher to share a funny story about a misbehaving kid in her class.

Shannon and I found each other, sitting on the stairs watching the annual Yankee Swap gift exchange. We were merely spectators as we didn't bring any gifts. Perhaps instead of going to the movies, we should have stopped off for hand lotion or scented candles. We sat there and whispered to each other as the Greenridge faculty took turns stealing the best bottle of wine and fanciest bath salts from each other. It was fun to make her laugh, and when it was genuine, Shannon had a great smile. *And those lips, my goodness!* Somehow she was youthful and sultry at the same time.

After helping Mr. Novak pick up wrapping paper off the floor, we decided to say our good-byes and call it an evening. The inside of my car was quiet as I drove to my place. Whether it was the size and scope of Jill's house or the reality of Sheri's divorced life, the evening was yet another reminder that everyone at the party was a life stage or two beyond me. At a red light, I looked over at Shannon in the passenger seat and I appreciated that she was close to my age. I probably looked a little too long.

"What?"

"Do you use much bath salt?" *I had to make up something.*

"I don't have a bathtub."

"I think there are fourteen bathtubs at Jill's place?'

"Did you see her bedroom? Her closet is bigger than a classroom."

"I'm sorry I don't have detailed knowledge of our assistant principal's sleeping quarters. What were you doing in her closet?"

"I guess she just had it renovated and she was showing it to Linda and a couple other teachers."

"Closet renovation? What does that even mean?"

"You know, like new shelves, custom shoe racks, and stuff."

As we continued to speculate on the specifics of overhauling one's closet, I pulled next to Shannon's car in my parking lot.

"Well, I'm sorry if that wasn't as exciting as your average college party."

"I'm done with college parties and tonight was fun. I'm glad we went."

"Me too."

"Good night." She smiled. And something in the way she smiled with her eyes seemed like an invitation. Acting with impulse, instead of my usual careful deliberation, I leaned over and gently pressed my lips against hers.

CHAPTER 9

VEGETABLE CREAM CHEESE

The next morning, I was slipping in between sleep and conscientiousness, inputting some of the content of my semi-lucid dreams. The setting was my sister's twelfth birthday party; Kelly was about to blow out the candles of a rainbow cake. While Kelly was at the height of her preteen awkward phase, her charm was evident, hiding behind an embarrassed smile as family and friends serenaded her. Though I would have been in high school at the time, I was watching the birthday party through the eyes of my adult self. *She was so young and had so much left to live for…*

Just about the time the cake was being cut, my brain definitively determined that this was a dream. My mind wandered from a birthday party over a decade ago to the events of the previous night. I opened my eyes to this morning's reality. *Holy shit! Did I kiss one of the student teachers last night?* I bolted straight up in bed and replayed the events in the parking lot again and again in my head; one minute we were talking and the next we were kissing. I hadn't planned it—it just happened.

And what does it mean?

Whoa, whoa, whoa! Let me stop you right there, Brain—we're not going down that road. As much as you love attributing significance to what's happened, let's not dissect this from every conceivable angle.

And what about Allie? One minute you think you're falling in love with the girl from middle school, the next you're locking lips with the student teacher?

Last night was fun. Shannon was fun. The kiss wasn't bad either.

Well…I guess we're going to consider it from some conceivable angles.

In my post-kiss clumsiness, I mumbled something about doing something over the weekend, and suddenly we had made plans for the next day—today. The only time Shannon was available was Saturday morning while she was on duty as a residence assistant. Since that required her to be in her dorm, she said I was welcome to come by and hang out. I suggested I could bring breakfast and, as suddenly as we had kissed, we had a second date.

After my shower, I eyeballed the mirror and contemplated what one wears to accompany someone who has RA "on call" dorm duty. I landed on a gray wool sweater, jeans, and trail shoes. With my olive barn coat, I looked like I could have been going for a hike. While I was certainly not a rugged nature enthusiast, Shannon seemed like the outdoorsy type.

As the car engine turned over, Kelly's mixtape resumed playing and it served as the soundtrack for the day's adventure. I tried to recall more details of my sister's twelfth birthday, and thinking of

Kelly distracted me from the foolishness of what I was doing today. Certain songs in the mixtape still hurt more than others, but their predictable sequence allowed me to manage the pain. I could brace myself for the sting of "There She Goes" because I knew it followed "Why Look at the Moon?" The comfortable last stains of "When it's Raining" were fading out by the time I reached the Superfresh grocery plaza. My plan was to stop at the bagel place on Route 27 because they had a great everything bagel, and then get coffees at Stan's, a food truck on campus, so they would be hot when I arrived.

It had been awhile since I had been in a dormitory. Without the necessary keycard, I followed two sophomore girls returning home from a jog into Harrington Hall, which made me feel old and creepy. The utilitarian, rectangular building with cinder block walls brought back fond memories of the protective bubble of being back in college. Shannon was on the third floor, and her door was held open with a two gallon jug of water. She was sitting on the world's smallest couch in a blue Rutgers sweatshirt with her hair in a ponytail reading a textbook. I stood in the doorframe and held up the brown paper bag and cardboard coffee holder like some sort of idiotic delivery man.

"Breakfast has arrived."

"You found me." Shannon stood up and tossed her book on the bed.

"The directions were excellent." I put the food down on a desk nearby. "I would have been here sooner, but I had to pick up all this extra stuff for the coffee." And I pointed to the creamers and sugars that were balanced in between the two styrofoam cups. Shannon mocked a laugh and playfully hit me on the arm. "All I'm saying, black coffee makes life easier."

"What did you bring me?"

"Bagels with vegetable cream cheese"

"Ooh…fancy."

"It's the only way I'm going to eat carrots and radishes."

I took a seat on the couch with my bagel wrapped in wax paper. Shannon went through the process of doctoring her coffee, and I attempted to watch her without staring. Shannon turned her desk chair around to face me. She held up one of New Jersey's best bagels, sliced in half with a ridiculously proportioned schmear in-between.

"That's a lot of cream cheese!"

"That's how they get a full serving of vegetables in there." Shannon then operated on her bagel with a plastic spoon, meticulously collecting cream cheese into a small Tupperware container before housing it in the door of a dented mini-fridge covered in Greenpeace and Amnesty International stickers. I admired the discipline with which she allocated equal parts of cream cheese on each half of her bagel, as well as determining what amount was meant to be kept in reserve.

"Later today or tomorrow with some pretzels, that will make an excellent snack," she announced like she was hosting a cooking show. I smiled at her resourcefulness.

In between sips of coffee, we made small talk, occasionally interrupted by sheepish undergraduates who were locked out of their rooms. She smiled sympathetically at each freshman and sophomore who showed up at her door, and based on her interactions, I could see she had that intangible interpersonal quality that makes you a good teacher.

"It was hard to book an audience with you. What else do you have going on this weekend?" I asked her.

"Tonight I'm going over to one of my professor's houses for dinner. She's having a bunch of her students over."

"Really? I never dined with any of my professors."

"Dr. Simmons? She's awesome! I love her. She is why I stayed with speech pathology."

"You majored in both?"

"Graduated in May with a double major, speech and education. Now, I'm just finishing up my master's in education."

Shannon's eyes lit up when she described a variety of people she had gotten to know over the past four years. She obviously wasn't there just for the grades; she had formed some real genuine relationships, with both professors and friends. Listening to her retell her time at Rutgers, I was a little jealous of her college experience. While I had incubated for four years at a more expensive private university, it dawned on me that Shannon was extracting far more value from her in-state public school tuition. Like harvesting the surplus cream cheese off a bagel, she savored every moment of this experience.

During one of Shannon's trips to unlock a door, I surveyed the artifacts in her room: a green mountain bike that needed new tires, a poster of Gustav Klimt's "The Kiss," lots of pictures of friends drinking out of plastic cups. In between the couch and her bed was a wooden crate, which was being used as a nightstand. Within a silver frame sat a picture of a couple at Rutgers tailgate decked out in black and red, embracing in the parking lot. I was holding it when Shannon returned to the room.

"Is this Craig?"

"Yes."

"Looks like you guys are having a good time?"

"That was before the Miami game last year. We were all excited because the number one team in the country was coming to New Brunswick. Of course, we went on to lose 55–6."

"Ouch. Big football fan?"

"I like going to the games. Even though Rutgers is really bad, it's kind of like a big party. Craig really loves football. He's excited because Nashville is going to get a pro team next year."

I paid closer attention to the lanky figure in the picture clutching the cute Irish girl with curly hair. Craig was an attractive guy: dark hair, dark eyes, well put together—without having that dull frat boy look about him. I could picture myself grabbing a beer and watching a football game with him. The details of their current relationship absolutely intrigued me, but I wasn't going to bring it up. While thinking about Glen with Allie made me absolutely jealous, I was merely curious about Craig. Last night's kiss was fairly innocent, but I still wanted to know how far I'd trespassed over some boundary. After a pause, Shannon offered the explanation I hadn't asked for.

"We started dating last year—friend of a friend sort of thing. Even though we were both seniors and he was going to Nashville, we never had *the* serious talk before graduation. We've been going back and forth since then, but it's not the same. He's come back for every home game; I've flown out to see him a bunch. He's sort of suggested I should move there at the end of this school year. Maybe it would be different if we lived in the same place…I don't know."

Still holding their picture in my hand, I suddenly ached for Shannon and Craig and almost wanted this cute couple to figure it out. *What should I say next? I have to demonstrate that I'm listening, while not asserting my own agenda or coming across as self-serving.* What came out of my mouth was safe and harmless.

"Distance is hard."

"Yeah," Shannon nodded and disappeared into her own thoughts. Her big eyes stared off into the distance for a memory or two. I, as well, thought about the distance in my life. After Thanksgiving, I probably would have dropped everything and moved to Boston, but getting to be with Allie was not without its own obstacles.

"What about you? You mentioned that girl from high school you saw over Thanksgiving? Holly?"

"Allie," I corrected. I guess it was my turn for relationship honesty. Apparently, we weren't going to directly talk about last night's kiss, but we were both going to find some context for it. "I've known her for years, even though we had drifted apart. She came to my sister's funeral. She's great, but she's in Boston." I heard the word "Boston" and the way I said it made it sound almost inaccessible, like it was some colony on the moon.

"You said she's a painter?'

"Yes."

And with that, everyone on the couch had disclosed any and all romantic entanglements. I don't think either of us planned for that to be on the breakfast agenda, but somehow it paved the way for what happened next. I wasn't thinking about it at the time, but I think Shannon and I both needed some level of honesty in order to move forward. Without saying it, we mutually and tacitly agreed to be each other's backup relationship.

Our silent compact was interrupted by a digital clock next to the tailgate picture signaling the end of Shannon's time as RA on duty. After resetting the alarm, Shannon got up, walked over to the door, and slid the water jug away with her left foot. The metal door of room #318 swung shut. Shannon softly latched the deadbolt and turned back toward me, her deep olive eyes locked on mine. My heartbeat quickened. She took deliberate steps in my direction and stopped in front of the couch. Her hands reached the bottom of her blue sweatshirt, and slowly, she pulled it over her head before tossing it in the direction of the mountain bike. There she stood, in her jeans and bra, arms at her side. The tiniest of exhales escaped from her lips.

Fingers reached out and found each other. I stood up and maintained eye contact as my left hand found the skin above her hip. She leaned her head backward so her hand could release the scrunchie holding her hair together. My hand traced upward as I planted my mouth on hers.

We had told each other that, to some degree, we were spoken for. But those loyalties lived in other times and in other cities. Right now, in Harrison Hall, Shannon and I formed a bond without complication or commitment. While we may not have been each other's first choice, we were each other's choice for the moment.

CHAPTER 10

THE LOVE PENTAGRAM

The day after breakfast, and other activities, with Shannon my mind went into overdrive overanalyzing the situation. What had I gotten myself into? What did I know about potentially juggling two women? Everything I knew about relationships involved serial monogamy. I was a notorious late bloomer and had nothing on my sexual resume through high school. When I got to college I didn't make up for lost time by hooking up with everyone, but instead by having a serious three-year relationship with Michelle. Then another long term relationship with Tara after college. Historically, I seemed to be wired for stable relationships. But how could I possibly pick one of these women when they were already picked by someone else? I was wrestling with all of this when Allie called me that night.

"Where are you?"

"I'm at home. What do you mean?"

"What I mean is that you're distracted. You're not really engaged in talking to me." Allie was right. Our phone conversation didn't have the usual light and flirtatious feel. Ever since Thanksgiving, talking to Allie on the phone made me feel like I was fourteen, stretching the kitchen wall phone cord into the living room, so I could have some modicum of privacy. But now, I could feel myself being distant with Allie.

"I've have to tell you something and I don't know exactly how to say it.'"

"Just tell me."

"Well...I've kind of started seeing someone."

Pause. Very long pause. I considered breaking the silence, but I knew it was absolutely Allie's turn to talk next.

"Who is it?"

"A student teacher at my school."

Another long pause.

"So she's young."

"She graduated last spr—," and I stopped, knowing no justification was necessary. "Allie, you know how I feel about you. I don't know if either of us knows exactly what our relationship is, but I wanted to be honest with you."

"I know." Allie exhaled and I could sense her confusion. "James, this is going to sound horrible, but I didn't expect to feel this way about you. I went to Kelly's funeral because I needed to, felt compelled to, but then I talked to you at the church...I don't know... it's like we were supposed to be there for each other."

"It feels...," I started without a complete thought, "...like...we reconnected for a reason and to be honest I think about it all the time. Maybe this particular chapter is not the one where we wind up together. You're in Boston and you're with Glen, but perhaps someday, you won't be in Boston and you won't be with Glen."

Longest pause yet.

"So many times, I've tried to tell myself that you and I are friends, but I can't keep us in that box, you know? Every time we talk, it's clear there's something more and I wasn't expecting you to tell me about somebody else. I'm sorry, James, I'm really confused."

"I know." We stayed on the phone for a long time, sometimes talking, but often pausing. Eventually, we managed to get the emotional tenor of the conversation back to neutral, agreeing to talk again before Christmas.

Hanging up the phone, I felt a sense of relief but not any more resolution. Obviously, I had felt guilty and needed to absolve myself by telling Allie about Shannon. I viewed the weekend's activities as a transgression of an imaginary committed relationship. But at the same time, it absolutely affected Allie. *Allie cared who I was dating.* So, while it's not the traditional boyfriend-girlfriend relationship, there is something between us; something growing that could be hurt if not nurtured properly. Still, Allie kissed me and hasn't shed herself of her existing relationship, so there's no way this could be considered exclusive. Right?

And was this fair to Shannon? Perhaps more importantly, what does "this" even mean in reference to Shannon? When you told Allie "I've started seeing someone," that was a bit of stretch; you hung out for a weekend.

Who knows where that's going? As I pondered over that possibility, I had to admit to myself, there was something exciting about it. In this bizarre romantic scenario I had found myself in, Shannon was the "other woman" and if I was being honest, I kind of liked that. That is, if Shannon is okay with this arrangement.

Any question about Shannon's participation was answered the following Monday when we arrived at school about the same time. We saw each other across the parking lot and seemingly synchronized our gaits to land at the crosswalk at the same time. She had on a black wool coat, but her complexion was already red from the cold.

"Good Morning!"

"How was your weekend?" I asked with a goofy over-the-top grin.

"It was really good." And she responded with the same stupid smile back to me. It wasn't a long exchange, but revealed everything. It was the cryptic code of two coworkers who now knew each other in a much more intimate way, the secret handshake of club members who had to maintain decorum in a public setting. I wanted so badly to reach out and hug her, but I had to settle for shared knowing looks as we walked past other members of the faculty.

I was able to sit on that secret for all of two days. Wednesday was the last day of school before Christmas vacation, and I ran to Sheri's room after the final bell because I had to tell someone. She was picking up the remains of a holiday class party when I burst into her room and closed her door. I rushed over to her and spilled the details of the Christmas party and the weekend. After taking it all in, Sheri went right into teacher mode.

"Let me see if I have this straight, you are a part of two distinct, yet separate love triangles." Sheri picked up a piece of chalk and jotted the letters "J," "A," and "G," on the chalkboard before connecting them with diagonal lines. She pointed the chalk at me and then touched the letter J. "So you're in love with Allie, who also has a boyfriend named Glen?" For the visual learners, Sheri tapped the initials of the names as she recited them.

"Correct." With the chalkboard skills of a classroom veteran, Sheri then drew the letters "S" and "C" on the other side of the J and connected them with alternating diagonal segments.

"Annnnnd," Sheri continued, "You recently hooked up with Shannon, who happens to have a college boyfriend named Craig?" She ended her question with the chalk pointing at the C.

"Also correct."

"So you're telling me there's these two guys, Glen and Craig, who are indirectly romantically linked to each other and they have no idea they're connected?"

"That may be the case."

Then dotting the chalk across the chalkboard, Sheri drew a perforated line connecting the G and C.

"Now," she said, summarizing her lesson, "If only somehow Glen and Craig could meet and start dating each other, you, sir, would truly be a part of an incredibly rare love pentagram." Sheri stood back, admiring the perfectly drawn geometric figure that modeled my love life.

"I'd say it's more of a pentagon." It was both amusing and flattering to have a friend take such interest in what was going on with me.

"Sure, but pentagram sounds more exciting than pentagon."

"Given."

"Well, divorced mother here, so I'm certainly no relationship expert, but this strikes me as a very unstable romantic structure." She drew a circle around her whole model. "What are you going to do?"

"I'm not entirely sure."

"If you want my advice, I'd say don't worry about figuring it out. No one is married. No one has any kids. You were honest with both women. Just enjoy yourself."

Tension rose in my body when Sheri bought up the marital and parental status of the initials on her chalkboard. Part of me took offense to the notion that the stakes of my life were perhaps lower than hers. As Sheri began packing up her work stuff, I looked at the framed photo of her kids on her desk and thought maybe she was right. After putting on her coat, Sheri ran an eraser over the geometry of my love life, like it was today's long division lesson.

"I've got to go get a few presents before picking up the kids. Have a great break and a very Merry Christmas."

"You too."

It was dark by the time I cleaned up my classroom and got to the parking lot, and the few cars that were left were covered with two inches of new snowfall. I was toting a bright red department store bag full of gifts from my students, mostly ties decorated with cartoon characters. There was just enough snow on the ground that each step made a muted crunch and left a distinctive sneaker print. Looking back at the dimly lit playground and baseball field, I watched the individual snowflakes passing in front of the streetlamps. My nose filled with the cold, clean scent of winter. I thought about the cleansing effect of new snow, how it blankets the world, somehow softening some of life's sharper edges. I placed my backpack and the bright red bag in the car, and decided to take a walk in the snow.

There was no traffic on Waller Street, no cars returning from work and not one child dragging a sled home from the neighborhood hill. Even the lights hanging on the one-story homes twinkled with a quiet modesty. While it was only three days before Christmas, everyone must have hunkered down or embarked on their holiday travel. With the exception of my footsteps, there was no sound; tonight the snow was heavy enough to absorb all the noise, including my thoughts. With each step, I strode deeper into a beautiful solitude, the only witness to this momentary peace.

The fleeting silence was broken by the sound of a motor. At first, two bright headlines and then an Ashford Park fire engine emerged into view. Its lights weren't flashing and the siren was off; it wasn't on its way to an emergency and no one in the neighborhood was about to have an awful Christmas. In fact, just the opposite. As the truck cut a path through the freshly laid powder, I made eye contact with a figure standing on the back of the fire truck: it was Santa Claus himself. He didn't say anything, but he waved to me as he rode by, and I held up my gloved hand in return. I looked around to see if anyone had seen this, but not a creature was stirring. I watched Santa's fire truck until the hum of the engine was swallowed by the snow and the darkness.

Now, I knew it probably wasn't the real St. Nicholas, probably just some overweight volunteer firefighter making a charity event appearance. Despite the fire truck originating from Station #3 and not the North Pole, it was a perfect moment nonetheless: the snow, the night, the quiet, and Fireman Santa whom only I saw. I looked back at the school's baseball field, now off in the distance, and determined there was enough magic in the air to make a Christmas wish: I wanted to have both Allie and Shannon in my life.

To hell with traditional dating; if both women were okay with this game, I was ready to play it. It seemed to me, based on what I'd been through, I deserved some fun and happiness.

In balancing the ledger of my life, as far as I was concerned, the universe fucking owed me, big time. Why shouldn't I be allowed to juggle two romances? Bring on the pentagram!

I exhaled deeply and watched as my breath dissipated against the blackness of the sky. After drinking in the moment, images of both Allie and Shannon floated through my brain followed by Sheri's chalkboard illustration of our relationships. As my sneaker made the first crunch back toward the parking lot, I felt a giddy smile forming on my face. I recalled a memory of my sister—the image of her high school senior photo full of locks of curly hair and her radiant, infectious smile—and the weight of her loss didn't feel quite as heavy. With Christmas only a few days away, I would somehow survive what had been the absolute worst year in my life; certainly next year would have to be better.

CHAPTER 11

DOING DISHES IN ALABAMA

I closed my book as soon as I heard rubber hitting the tarmac. Looking out the window, I watched the rehearsed choreography of ground crews directing planes and maneuvering luggage. Rolling toward C25, I had no idea what to expect this first Christmas since Kelly died. I had called an audible and decided not to go home to see my parents for the holidays. As a child of divorce, having to endure the two Christmas dinners, one with each parent, was taxing enough. Not only is there a limit to how much spiral-cut ham one can eat, I was in no mood to do this year's dance combined with the additional dead sister challenge. I had told my mom that it was really important that I spend some time with my sister Jackie and, while disappointed, she was thankful her children were together for the holidays. So, I booked a flight to Nashville, which was the closest airport to where my sister called home.

Years earlier, after telling my parents that their three-year investment into college was not for her, my older sister ran away from home. One day, she got in her car and drove far enough away that it would be too hard to go back. When the car finally stopped, it was in Huntsville, Alabama. Since then, she had not been back for birthdays, holidays, or anything. When Kelly died, we hadn't seen each other in over three years.

Yet, there wasn't a hint of uneasiness when I hopped inside her Dodge Neon outside the Nashville Airport. We were born sixteen months apart and had a reservoir of experiences and common language we could always fall back on. She was the older sister, the leader, the one who had a better feel of how to navigate our parents, whether trying to avoid punishment or negotiating a later bedtime. I was the entertainer, who would make Jackie laugh at inappropriate times until my mom would invariably chastise her, "Stop encouraging him!"

For years, Jackie and I were responsible for cleaning up the kitchen after dinner and we unintentionally bonded over the nightly routine. As I started clearing the dishes, Jackie would go into the living room and put a record on our dad's turntable. Many nights, it would be The Beatles' *Sgt. Peppers*. The fake audience in the opening eponymous track added energy and levity to the task of cleaning up my mom's cream of mushroom soup casseroles. With my older sister scrubbing out pots and me loading the dishwasher, we would duet "With a Little Help from My Friends." We could usually be finished and wiping down the countertops by the first chorus of "Fixing a Hole."

Our taste in music and sense of humor were two things that my older sister and I always shared. After Kelly's funeral, we started sending each other postcards with song lyrics on it. No salutation, no other message, just one line of a song we thought the other might appreciate. You could say it was our version of trading mixtapes. "Loser" by Beck was pumping out of the car stereo as we headed south on 65.

"So Allie is one of the girls you're dating? Kelly's friend Allie?" Jackie was dramatically aghast as she looked in the mirror before switching lanes.

"Technically, she was my friend before she was Kelly's friend."

"Excuse me. And the other woman?"

"She just finished her student teaching at my school."

Without the visual aid of a chalkboard drawing, I walked my sister through the love pentagram. We compared notes on which gifts we sent Mom and Dad. I looked over at Jackie in the driver's seat, with trees passing behind her, and while she definitely looked older, there was a sameness to her that I had known all my life. The conversation flowed freely and the silences were never awkward. We picked back up just like when we were kids.

The sun was setting by the time we arrived at my sister's place, a modest three-bedroom house she was renting with her boyfriend. With his long hair and relaxed demeanor, Kevin looked like a keyboard player for a Journey cover band. He was quiet and easy to be around. The three of us talked and drank into the evening until Jackie determined she was calling it a night.

"You know some of us have to work tomorrow," she announced, grabbing some empty beer bottles off the coffee table. Looking at Kevin, she asked, "So, what will you two do tomorrow?"

"Probably head out to Big Spring or Redstone," Kevin replied casually. I had no idea what that meant.

"Take good care of my baby brother," Jackie warned somewhat jokingly. Kevin smiled and took a sip of his beer.

Big Spring turned out to be a disc golf course, a series of eighteen "holes" players navigated with specialized Frisbees or discs, which you finished by landing your disc within the hanging chains of a metal basket. Jackie hadn't told me much about Kevin besides that when he wasn't bartending, he was playing disc golf and smoking pot. The Big Spring parking lot resembled the trailhead of a hike, a few dirt spots surrounded by oaks and laurels that had shed their leaves for winter. When we arrived, Kevin reached into the glove compartment and pulled out a sealed plastic bag with several joints. Taking one out, he lit it with a red plastic lighter, drew on it, and then offered it to me.

I pinched the paper and inhaled without hesitation. During the ride from the airport, Jackie had informed me about the prospect of getting high with her boyfriend. In the vein of *the universe owed me, why not settle part of that debt with some hedonism in Huntsville?* For the next three or four songs, we smoked as Kevin laid out the basics of disc golf. For starters, the discs aren't like the Frisbees you toss around at the beach; they're smaller, denser, and harder to throw straight. Just like traditional golf, there are particular discs you use to "drive," "approach," or "putt."

After a few holes, my throws were getting the S-shaped flight path Kevin had told me about. In my altered state, watching the spinning orange disc carve to the right before softly falling to the left was a thing of beauty, a miracle of physics. My driver was called "the leopard" (they're all named after animals for some reason) and once it launched, time would freeze and there was only 175 grams of plastic hurdling, circling, and dancing toward its intended destination.

As we hiked through the Alabama woods, the pot kept me centered in sensations of the park: the bright colors of the discs, the smell of aging leaves, the occasional rattling of metal chains when discs hit their targets. It was a welcome escape not to have my mind littered with thoughts of the past and future. Like any good vacation, this trip was a diversion from my normal life, which had been colored with incredible sadness for the past few months. My outing to Big Spring was a success (not sure what would have amounted to failure) and Kevin offered to take me out to a new course the next day. This became my daily Huntsville routine: wake up, get stoned, play disc golf.

After each disc golf outing, we'd meet back up with Jackie in the early evening. When she returned home from her waitressing job, Kevin would be smoking pot and playing Doom on his computer while I napped on their couch, recovering from my increased marijuana intake and elevated physical activity. Once awake, Jackie would ask me, "How are you doing?" with the appropriate concern of an older sister. Her daily question was probably about how well I was adapting to my "Huntsville wake-and-bake disc golf" lifestyle, but on Christmas Eve, the question landed differently.

"Hey, how are you doing?"

"I miss her."

"I know. I do, too."

"Do you remember when we were teaching her to write her name…"

"And she started writing 'Ks' all over the house?" My sister completed my thought and I was glad she remembered. "Little scribbly uppercase Ks in random places all over the walls. Very small and in very faint pencil. We would keep finding new ones. She was the Zorro of Westfield Drive."

"And she didn't get in trouble because she was the youngest." I sat up and specifically remembered one of the initials on the stairway down to the basement. We both laughed at that and then, whether it was nostalgia or the remains of cannabis in my system, a string of thoughts started associating: *the uppercase Ks…Kelly learning to write her name…Kelly writing her name for the last time…the suicide letter.*

The police had found it, a crumpled up page from a spiral notebook thrown in the trash, like it was a rough draft. And if it wasn't the last version, what wasn't finalized: the wording or the choice to commit suicide? It hurt like hell that my sister had killed herself, but there was a whole other layer of pain to know that as the author of her own death she was potentially unsure of how she wanted her story told. Plus, a final insult: *why wasn't I mentioned in the letter?* The rest of my family's names appeared in Kelly's explanation and apology, yet mine was absent. Of all the unanswered questions around my sister's death, this is the one that tied me in most mental knots. On this night, the knots were tied tightly enough to produce tears.

Jackie got up from her chair and draped her arm around me. Like she always had, my big sister took care of me. Once again, we were children sitting on the big rock in the backyard of our new house after we moved to a strange neighborhood. Back then, Jackie quelled my fears by sharing her bag of M&Ms and letting me eat all the green ones. Now, the big rock was replaced by a beat up leather couch and instead of M&Ms there were light beers in the fridge, but the feeling remained the same. As Jackie held me, her protective, nurturing nature enveloped me. I was safe.

When I woke up on Christmas morning, the aroma of coffee and cinnamon filled the small house. As I walked down the hallway from the guest bedroom, I could see that their small dining table had been set with precision: patterned tablecloth, green ceramic plates, and hand-me-down crystal juice glasses. In the middle of each plate, was a bowl with a halved grapefruit, each adorned with half a maraschino cherry.

"Merry Christmas!" My sister was taking something out of the oven. I looked again at the grapefruits and wanted to cry, but this time not out of sadness. The grapefruits and the freshly-baked cinnamon rolls meant Jackie was recreating our traditional childhood Christmas breakfast, the one we had every year before opening presents. It was the best gift I could have received.

"Merry Christmas," I finally said after a while. Still stunned, I saw the pie plate on the counter, crust protected with tin foil surrounding beautifully browned eggs. It was my mom's quiche Lorraine, which we ate only once a year. I looked at my sister in amazement and tried to acknowledge her efforts, "You made…"

"Yep," and she gave me a wink.

Kevin put some Christmas carols on the stereo and the three of us toasted juice glasses. Sitting in my sister's modest breakfast nook, I felt a sense of family and belonging that I hadn't in a long time. At the time of the funeral, there were lots of family and friends around trying to provide comfort, but being bonded in misery is different from enjoying each other's company. I had been worried about this Christmas and how I would handle it. There were no gifts for Kelly or from Kelly under the tree, that was sure, but her absence at the holidays was softened by spending this time with my other sister. Reaching for another cinnamon roll, I was thankful Jackie had welcomed me into her world and brought comforts from our childhood with her. We had a leisurely breakfast, joking and telling stories for a good portion of the morning.

After the meal was over, I started clearing the table and Jackie swapped out Bing Crosby for some Grateful Dead. As "Box of Rain" bounced off the walls of the tiny house, my older sister and I did the dishes.

CHAPTER 12

THE NEW YEAR

The protective haze of disc golf, marijuana, and sisterly guidance enveloped me for almost two weeks before the siren song of elementary school began calling. As much as I enjoyed walking stoned through the woods with Kevin, I couldn't maintain this lifestyle for too much longer—even baked out of mind at 10:30 in the morning, somehow I knew this wasn't who I normally was. (I did buy some of my own discs and used an AOL account to look up disc course locations in New Jersey.) On the drive back to Nashville airport, Jackie continued her investigation on how I was going to proceed romantically in the new year.

"So you're not going to try to have a relationship with one of them?" tilting her head toward me.

"Not right now. Just my luck to find two girls already in somewhat committed relationships." Jackie smiled and I continued, "Right after Kelly's funeral, I would have quit my job and moved to Boston for Allie. But…she's got a life and a boyfriend, so I'm trying to be with her however I can. At the same time, spending time with Shannon is just fun and easy. After what you and I have been through, I feel like we deserve some fun and easy."

Jackie nodded and observed, "So you've got it all figured out?"

"Oh…absolutely not."

We both laughed in unison and the conversation stalled. This time together reminded me how much I missed my older sister and how much I needed her in my life. As we got off the highway, I spotted that Jackie had one or two gray hairs, a sign that we might actually be grown-ups. Eleven years after Jackie decided to leave college, it dawned on me that she accomplished the thing you're supposed to do while you're there—grow up and find yourself. This Huntsville version of my sister was happy and content; free of some of the turmoil that she had wrestled with previously. On the curb of Terminal 2 Jackie left me with one last piece of advice.

"Safe travels. Be careful." It was generic advice, but I knew from her tone that the subtext was Allie and Shannon.

"I will."

"I love you."

"I love you, too." We hugged one last time and my Christmas vacation came to an end.

It was comforting to return to the world of reading groups and bell schedules as Room 22 hit the ground running at the start of January. Energized from my time off and experiencing greater clarity from my prolonged walks in the woods, I was up before the alarm sounded and my car was the first in the parking lot. My students responded to my enthusiasm, and with the holidays behind them, their little brains were focused and hungry to learn. We breezed through *Frog and Toad Are Friends*, performed an entertaining "sink or float" science experiment, and absolutely crushed a math unit on picture graphs.

Shannon was no longer at Greenridge as the holidays corresponded with the end of her semester of student teaching. She was back at Rutgers taking classes for her master's, and I missed stealing glances of her face and figure around the hallways. She would come over to my place for dinner, and we'd get Indian take-out and watch TV. If I knew Shannon was coming over, I would make an attempt at cleaning up: moving dishes from the sink to the dishwasher and hiding piles of clothes in the closet. As soon as she walked in the door, her smile lit up my drab apartment and added light to my life. I'd update her on the current events at Greenridge and she'd entertain me with stories of undergraduates doing dumb things. Other times, she'd do homework on the couch while I graded papers on the dining table.

Thursday nights were the perfect night for our Indian take-out. Not only was the lineup on NBC incredibly strong, Shannon also didn't have any classes on Friday, which meant it was easy for her to spend the night. And for the sake of juggling, Thursday night was also the night Allie taught an art class at a community college, so it was very unlikely she would call. Just because I was trying to date two women, didn't mean it wouldn't be incredibly awkward if their worlds collided. These were the pentagram problems. On

Friday morning, Shannon and I would share coffee and cereal before parting ways.

By Sunday, my attention would shift, as the best time to catch Allie on the phone was right around the time *60 Minutes* came on the air. Our conversations had an otherworldly, ethereal feel to them. I didn't allow my mind to wander, staying completely focused on her and her voice. It had this soft, sweet quality to it that made me want more of her, made me want to be right there with her. Sometimes, I had this inkling that the next words out of Allie's mouth were going to be that Glen was no longer be in the picture, but my premonitions never came to fruition. Once she did bring up Glen, but it was a matter of logistics.

"Did you say you have time off in February?" she asked.

"I have a five-day weekend around President's Day." The phone went still after my seemingly innocuous response about my schedule. "Allie?" After summoning enough courage, she eventually posed the question she wanted to ask.

"What do you think about coming to see me?"

"What about—"

"Glen's going on a ski trip with his brothers." *Hell yeah! Glen's going on a ski trip! And, by the way, it appears Allie can do a bit of relationship juggling herself.* My heart leapt with the excitement of getting accepted into college. I gave a fist pump in the kitchen that almost knocked over the pan of chicken I was cooking. I composed myself before accepting her invitation.

"That would be great."

With the Boston trip on the schedule, Allie and I started to supplement our phone communication by exchanging letters. This correspondence wasn't describing the pedestrian events of our daily lives; these were romantic missives full of flowery language and heart-on-sleeve sentiment. I was banking on the fact that Glen, the computer programmer, couldn't string together eloquent prose the way I could. As Allie was a painter, why not try to woo her with some of that right-brained creativity she delves into for her artwork?

I created a whole ritual around writing Allie from the surface of my father's old metal desk. After lighting a few candles, I would prop up a photograph Allie she had sent me against the base of a lamp. Going into one of the metal drawers, I would get out the stationary set that I shelled out nearly twenty dollars at a local Princeton boutique, a major upgrade from a yellow legal pad. Lastly, I would retrieve the fountain pen from the engraved wooden case someone gifted me for graduation, which previously I never thought to use.

Feeling the thickness and texture of the expensive paper brought to mind the movie *Roxanne*, which Kelly and I both adored. In particular, a scene in which Steve Martin's character, C.D., begins writing romantic letters on behalf of a word-clumsy coworker; he needs to gain inspiration from his instruments and searches for a good pen. I laughed to myself and recited the line out loud that Kelly and I had quoted to each other dozens of times.

"And some good quality paper that really takes the ink."

It was a throwaway line from a silly movie that for whatever reason resonated with Kelly and me. So, whenever something involved paper, pens, or writing, we gratuitously tried to work that snippet of Steve Martin's script into the conversation. It was somewhat childish, but it was part of the shared vernacular that fed our relationship. Sometimes, a memory of Kelly would spiral me into despair; other times, I would be able to find a small nugget of happiness among the sensation of loss. On this night, the memory was bittersweet. I fondly remembered all the times we watched *Roxanne* on HBO and the original movie poster I was able to locate for her birthday one year.

Like C.D. Bales, I sat and tried to craft the perfect words for the feelings I had for the object of my affection. One night, in a moment inspired by the pen or the "good quality paper," I closed a letter with, "Even though you're far away, I know your heart lies just at the other end of this sentence." And I was pretty impressed with myself. In another writing session, I was mired in an attempt to describe the possibilities of our relationship. After crumpling up a horrible first-person account, what came out was a crude attempt of a poem:

between you and me
there is a bridge
connecting our hearts
despite distance and time
when the fog rolls in
the span disappears
all I can see is
an ocean between us
without map or compass
I'll again find my way
and walk to the middle
hoping you return

I felt like a hopeless romantic, or more accurately, *like an idiot.* Ultimately, I figured if I could pen the "heart at the end of the sentence" line, I could dabble in a little poetry. With trepidation, I put my verse into an envelope and mailed it. To my surprise, a week later Allie responded with a poem of her own:

A drop of water,
one of many in the stream,
finds its way
flowing
falling
rushing over rocks.
Until it reaches a bridge
spending a moment
a witness to a kiss
that took years to ever happen.

I couldn't believe it! *Allie sent me a bridge poem of her own. She had to be into me. There's no way Allie was writing poetry for the other guy. Some day she would come to her senses, drop Glen, and be with me.* Granted, Allie was a much better English student than I was back in high school. While I was lost in Mrs. Barron's lectures on *The Great Gatsby*, Allie was the star of the class, explaining Daisy's character while sketching trees in her notebook. So, there was a possibility I was misinterpreting her words. *But, come on!*

The next time we spoke on the phone, we didn't talk about poetry right away. Allie led a discussion of some of the things we could do together in Boston. We both may have been uncomfortable with the writers who had sent those letters—braver, bolder versions of ourselves, using the written word to say things to each other that we couldn't speak out loud.

I wanted to bring it up but I was wary of my reflective nature and incessant need to create meaning that had the tendency to be a "destroyer of moments." *Maybe we weren't meant to talk about the poems?* At the very least, I knew I had to start the conversation with something better than, "Hey, I really liked your poem." Finally, after a lull in the Boston planning, I ventured into waters with honesty and sincerity.

"You are an amazing writer."

"Thanks. You're not so bad yourself."

Even though Allie couldn't see me, I nodded my head, once and then again slowly. I raised my eyebrows, waiting, hoping for her to say something, waiting for her to explain feelings, to be the person who wrote the bridge poem. My heart was thumping so loud that I worried Allie could hear it through the phone. In the end, there would be no literary analysis of the two poets, no dissection of the art through a critical lens. We had acknowledged that those portions of our hearts existed and that would have to be enough. Part of me expected me to blurt out, "I love you!" right then and there. But I was able to hold back and choreograph a more nuanced, subtle version of this dance around each other.

After getting off the phone, I let my mind spin out of control well into the future, well beyond the February trip to Boston. *Would Allie and I wind up living in Boston, New Jersey, or maybe back home in New York? Would we move in together right away? Would we buy a house in our old home town? If so, could we afford to live in the school district we grew up in?*

In the middle of planning our inevitable future together, I thought back to Jackie's curbside advice to "be careful," which I knew I wasn't following. My last string of thoughts was reckless and irresponsible fantasies. I didn't care. Someday, Allie and I were going to be together.

CHAPTER 13

ON THE COUCH

Shannon rolled down the window of her Chevy Cavalier and prompted me by nudging my left arm. I passed her the turnpike ticket and ten dollars to pay for the route from Exit 9 to 13A. Returning the change, she asked which airline I was flying to, and I pointed out the next turn she needed to make. Based on our relationship (if you could call it that), it was reasonable for Shannon to give me a ride to the airport. It was, in my mind, a bit unusual that she was helping me catch a plane to go see another woman.

I had been open and honest with Shannon. As soon as I bought the ticket, I told her I was going to see Allie over President's Day weekend. It wasn't until a few days before the trip that we had a conversation about coordinating transportation over dinner at a Mexican restaurant.

"How are you getting to the airport?" Shannon asked after a sip of margarita.

"I figured I would take my car and park at the airport."

"That's crazy to spend money on that. Just let me drive you."

"Really?"

"Why not?"

"Because I'm going to—"

"Yeah, yeah, yeah, you're going to see Allie from high school and you've already picked out what shirt you're going to wear on the plane for when she sees you. Big deal. Wouldn't you drive me to the airport if I was flying to Nashville?"

"I guess?" I hadn't really considered the possibility.

"It's settled then." Shannon's willingness to help me get to Boston kind of amazed me, and her pragmatism had saved me $17.75 a day in parking.

When we got to the curb, Shannon stayed behind the wheel while I hopped out of the passenger seat. I was relieved she didn't get out of the car, because I wasn't sure what the appropriate goodbye would be. *Do you kiss or hug one pentagram dance partner as you're on your way to see the other?* We settled on waving through an open window and Shannon pulled away. As I stood outside the terminal, I noted the in-betweenness of getting out of Shannon's car on my way to drop in on Allie's life.

For the one-hour-and-eighteen-minute flight, I could barely contain my pent-up anticipation within seat 26D. *What would happen over the next four days? How would we do with this much time together? What would we say to each other? Was there a possibility that we may—*. I was so lost in my thoughts I almost spilled ginger ale on my new favorite shirt. Eventually, the plane landed at Logan, and I impatiently waited for the first twenty-five rows to exit before me. Allie said she would meet me at the gate. (Before 9/11, you didn't need a ticket to go through security.) As I walked down the Jetway, my heart was beating with excitement and suspense knowing that Allie was on the other side of the door. When my eyes found her, it was as magical as finding her in the gym after the funeral, but even more exciting.

She was dressed in a flannel shirt over a ribbed white turtleneck and light blue jeans. Her hair was down and draped over her arm was a winter coat, because it was February in Boston. It took my breath away to gaze upon the woman who had been writing me letters. We hugged and shared a brief kiss. Allie did not mention my shirt.

Home for Allie was a brick walk up in an up-and-coming South End neighborhood. Her second floor apartment was filled with stacked canvases everywhere, paintings in various degrees of completion. The living room was furnished with an eclectic combination of modern furniture and antiques. In the corner was an old armchair, which I think I sat in for a game of charades once when it lived in her parents' living room. Next to the charades chair was an antique side table holding books and a push-button phone. I pictured Allie sitting in the charades chair, with her legs curled under her, talking to me during one of our Sunday night conversations.

"Hey, I've got to talk to you about something." Her tone got remarkably serious as she interrupted my Sunday night phone visualization. We sat down on the couch in unison, and I braced myself.

"Okay."

"I'm really happy you are here." Allie's colorless greeting reminded me of a front desk hotel employee and made me a bit nervous as to what was coming next. "I want you here and I want to spend time with you. But I've thought a lot about this and although I invited you to stay here, I am not ready to share a bed with you. It's not a line I'm ready to cross." Her eyes never wavered as she got out her premeditated statement that had obviously been on her mind.

While disappointed, I wasn't completely surprised. In planning the trip, we never specifically addressed this. To this point, our relationship existed in a pretend state, an imaginary world of dreamy long-distance phone calls and romantic fantasies. The matter of who sleeps in which bed is a real world logistical matter. Now that we were together in person, these were some of the less-than-fairy-tale discussions we would have to have. It turns out we were sitting on what would be my bed for the weekend.

"I understand," I said, trying to put her mind at ease.

"Thank you." Allie reached her hand out to take mine, and her touch was filled with so much electricity, it instantaneously dilated our pupils, and no sooner were we in the midst of a heavy make-out session. Holding, groping, breathing heavily was a much-needed release of sexual tension that had been building for months. No clothes were removed, and we both seemed to know where we were supposed to stop. Afterward, I held her against my chest and felt the contours of her hip, our breathing patterns synchronizing. Something funny popped into my head, and just like in middle school, I couldn't not share it with Allie.

"Can I tell you something?" She picked up her pretty face to meet mine. "That was nice and all, but this is my bed, and there's certain lines I don't want to cross while we're in it." Allie reached for a pillow and smacked me in the head with it. I was glad she appreciated my sarcasm, and we laughed until she collapsed her head against me.

"I'm kind of hungry. Do you want to go get something to eat?"

"Sounds good. What's good around here?"

"Within a walk of here, there's a good Chinese place, an upscale diner, and an Irish tavern." When I heard 'Irish tavern,' a fleeting thought of Shannon came and went.

"The diner sounds good."

"It is. Sometimes I go there, get a cup of tea, and sketch for a couple hours."

"Cool. Dinner's on me." Even though I was a humble public school teacher, I was pretty sure that I made more money than Allie. Out of some chivalrous motive, I thought I should shoulder the larger part of funding the weekend.

"Sure. We're going to be spending a lot of time together—doing things, going out to eat. You can get dinner, I'll get the next thing, and we'll go dutch for the weekend."

"Seems abundantly fair."

"Okay. Give me like two minutes."

With the sleeping and financial arrangements for the next four days settled, Allie sprang off the couch and went to get ready. Holding my glasses up to the light, I could see they were smudged from their close brush with Allie's neck—an occupational hazard of being a nearsighted kisser. Smirking, I cleaned them off with my new favorite shirt.

Hub City Kitchen was exactly as Allie described it: a sleek, hip version of a 1950s diner. Black with teal accents and a bit of neon decor. We were led to a booth and sat across from each other just smiling.

"What?" Allie asked, breaking our smiling contest.

"I'm just happy to be here, happy to be with you." Allie broke out into an even bigger smile. She let me drink in her gaze for a brief instant and then her blue eyes surveyed the interior of the restaurant.

"I like the feel of this place. Kind of reminds me of The Pitchfork back home."

"Yes, I could see that." Casually looking around I added, "I couldn't tell you the last time I had salt potatoes."

A troubled look crossed Allie's face that I could tell had nothing to do with the timing of my last serving of the Central New York side dish. "I remember we were there after something sophomore year, maybe homecoming. Your mom was going to pick us up. You kept running to the pay phone to ask her if we could stay later and later, adding people to her car who she needed to take home. She was not too happy when she pulled up in the family station wagon at about eleven o'clock."

"I do remember that. I think that night provided me with a lot of motivation for me to get my license as soon as possible." Allie's expression deepened even further.

"Pretty soon after that, you and I didn't really hang out as much—"

"I know." I thought about the blue station wagon that became my first car, the freedom that came with driving, and how I used none of that freedom to drive over to Allie's house. Ever since Kelly's funeral, it was on my mind: how we drifted apart and now somehow drifted back together. We ordered food and held hands until Allie furrowed her brow in preparation of a serious inquiry.

"Can I ask you a question about Kelly?"

"Yes."

"How are you dealing with it?" It was a short question asked honestly and earnestly. There was compassion in her face, not the clinical inquisitiveness of a therapist. The question rolled around my brain, and I raised my eyes trying to locate the answer. With so many other people, I would have tossed out a flippant response like "with a steady diet of booze and denial," but I didn't have to use humor to protect my heart from Allie.

"Better, but not great. When it happened, my life was wrecked. There was nothing else—just a void, nothing. It still hurts more than I can talk about, but I'm finding ways to get up in the morning." Allie nodded and squeezed one of my hands harder.

"One of the reasons I ask is that I'm still having a really hard time with it. I'll be painting, and Kelly will come to mind, and I just can't believe she's gone."

"I'm sorry." I gave Allie's hand a squeeze in return.

Most of the time, when someone spoke about their experience following Kelly's death, I dismissed their grief because obviously mine was far greater. Why should anyone try to suggest they were feeling a loss that was even remotely in the same ballpark as mine? Besides my parents and sister, no one was beating me in the anguish department. But sitting across from Allie in the Hub City Diner, I empathized with her experience of losing a friend from childhood, who happened to be my sister. The conversation stretched out through a leisurely meal, culminating with a shared piece of pie, before we strolled back to her place.

Once home, bed sheets and pillows were retrieved from a closet. Allie put the sheets on the couch and topped them with a quilt that her mother had made. We kissed goodnight and I watched every step of her as she walked off to her bedroom. I placed my glasses and watch on a coffee table and reflected on the day's travels as well as our journey since October. Every moment I spent with Allie told me she was who I was supposed to be with. As I heard her stirring in the room next door, I knew I was head-over-heels completely in love with her. She made me feel light and open. I pulled Mrs. Lockwood's quilt over me and took stock of where I was. Moonlight through the window illuminated the room, and I could make out the rough outline of the charades chair and antique table in the corner. I was ecstatic about where I was and excited about where we were going.

CHAPTER 14

DINNER IN THE SUBURBS

After two dreamy days in Boston, Sunday morning found us in a pastry shop, enjoying chocolate croissants and French press coffee. Like the weekend itself, the setting of Douceur de Paris was perfect: the orderly rows of éclairs, the spotless shine of the marble tables, even the symmetrical mustache of the man behind the counter. Everything was magical with Allie; it was like she was some kind of witch who cast a spell on the whole city of Boston. Wherever we went, everyone around us—waiters, riders on the T, children on the street—seemed to smile upon us, as if they were extras in our own romantic comedy. I was amusing Allie by drawing funny figures on the fogged up window when she made me an interesting offer.

"How would you feel about having dinner with my sister's family tonight?" *Whoa. Stop the presses. Did I just receive an invite to meet Allie's family? Sure, I knew her parents back in the day, but we were never really dating, so this seemed much more significant.*

"That sounds great. Where do they live?" I asked nonchalantly.

"In Melrose; we'll have to drive there."

"So, who all are you parading me in front of?" I leaned back in my chair confidently. Allie playfully hit my knee, snapping me back into a less ridiculous posture.

"My sister, Melissa, her husband, Bill, and my nephews. Justin and Michael."

"Family audition, huh? You must really like me?" Allie retreated behind a coy smile.

"Or maybe Melissa's just been bugging me to return a dress I borrowed."

"I can wait in the car."

"Knock it off."

"How old are your nephews?"

"Almost five and three. They're pretty shy so don't expect too much interaction. They take a long time to warm up to new people, especially Justin." While Allie didn't work in the world of early childhood education, she had unknowingly thrown down the gauntlet with the challenge of shy kids about the age of my students. *Game on!*

As we drove out to the suburbs, I assumed Allie must have built this dinner into the schedule on a contingency basis. She always spoke reverently about Melissa, who was ten years older and whose opinion obviously carried a great deal of weight. It was easy to imagine that if anything was going to happen between Allie and me, it would hinge on earning her big sister's approval. I envisioned Allie quietly calling her sister from the privacy of her bedroom and giving the green light to dinner. Things had gone well, and now I got a chance to trek out to Melrose for pork tenderloin and risotto. As we drove over the Charles, I flashed Allie a little smile, letting her know I was on to her game.

Melissa and her family lived in a rust-colored colonial with a well-manicured lawn flanked by pine trees. Bill greeted us at the door, hugging his sister-in-law and offering me a firm "Hi, I'm a financial planner" kind of handshake. Melissa waved from the kitchen as she was obviously in a critical stretch of dinner preparation. Allie hugged Justin and Michael, who were sitting on a nearby staircase.

"Boys, this is my friend James. Can you say 'hi'?" I waved at the gallery on the stairs. Not a word. Michael was focused on rolling the wheels of a toy train; Justin stared right through me with his dark brown eyes.

"They're still groggy from a nap," Bill explained, "James, what are you drinking?" Bill went to retrieve me a beer; Melissa emerged from the kitchen wiping her hands on a tea towel. She looked just like Allie, but a decade older. Her blonde hair had been conformed into a "mom" haircut, and a few more wrinkles had taken hold of her face. She gave me a hug like we've known each other for years.

"It's great to see you," Melissa said, clutching my left arm, "I remember when you and Allie were both in the middle school musical."

"That's too bad. I was hoping everyone had forgotten that production of *Bye Bye Birdie*." Melissa laughed heartily and excused herself to work on dinner. Bill returned with two of the latest seasonals from Sam Adams, gave them to Allie and me, and returned to the kitchen to help. Allie sat next to Justin on the stairs and engaged him in the book he was holding.

With the sounds of stirring and chopping in the background, I took a sip of my beer and looked at the family photo above the brick fireplace. Examining the Walkers in their coordinated denim shirts, it was uncanny how similar Allie looked like her older sister. Based on Melissa's warm hug and generous laughter, she seemed receptive to the boy from her hometown trying to date her sister. Perhaps Glen hadn't won over their hearts and...*he hadn't found the key to unlock the shy nephews!* I knew what I had to do, and I scanned the room to find something to help me complete my mission. Next to the overstuffed couch was a built-in shelf, storing toys and books. Lying on hardwood floors below were more toy trains and a par-tially completed puzzle—*Bingo!*

A wooden tray puzzle with a brightly painted farm was going to be my hook. Only one of the animal pieces, the horse, had been cor-rectly put in place. I sat down in front of the couch and examined the puzzle, as if it were one of the great mysteries of the universe. Feigning confusion, I picked up the cow by its wood peg handle and started trying it in all the wrong spaces. As my fake confusion grew, I tapped the wood harder, which got the attention of Michael. The wheels of his train stopped spinning, and my Jedi teacher sense could tell he was now watching. The younger boy took the bait and got off the stairs, causing Allie to stop reading mid-sentence.

Michael plopped down in front of me, like a supervisor inspect-ing the work of one of his reports. I tapped the cow a few more times before looking at the young boy with a confused expression. I shrugged my shoulders as if to say *I can't figure this one out*. Michael took a couple draws on his pacifier before responding to my questioning eyes. A little finger emerged from the sleeve of his onesie pajamas, and he pointed to a cow-shaped hole in the left-hand corner of the puzzle. Maintaining eye contact, I carefully brought the cow to its resting spot and breathed a sigh of relief.

"Thanks," I said as if Michael had performed some miracle. I picked up another piece, this time a chicken, and again went through the pretense of not knowing what to do with it. This time, I took my act to a whole new level, trying the puzzle piece not only on the farm tray, but also on other puzzles, books, and objects around the room. Really getting into the character, I held the chicken up to a lamp and sincerely asked, "Do you think it goes here?" to which Michael laughed, almost losing his pacifier. His younger brother's level of amusement was enough for Justin to detach from Allie's reading and come check it out.

Before long, I had both boys careening around the living room, trying wooden puzzle pieces in places they absolutely didn't belong, cracking themselves up at the futility of the exercise. Without making eye contact with her, I could tell Allie was clearly entertained by the show I was putting on. Sure—some of it was for her benefit, but I genuinely enjoyed entertaining her nephews. At the same time, if playing with Justin and Michael earned me any favor with their aunt, I wasn't going to complain.

Before dinner, Allie gave me a very slow, sweet kiss on the cheek. The way her hand lingered on my shoulder in the wake of her lips made me shiver. *Might this be the night?* We all sat down at a comfortable table next to the kitchen. Melissa occupied herself cutting the boys' food and wiping applesauce off their faces. The boys took turns singing songs, and sometimes their parents joined in. It was a very different model of adulthood compared to the scene at the Greenridge Christmas party. Jill's house seemed like a museum of upward mobility; this house was a testament to an actual loving family. When the appropriate amount of chicken nuggets had been consumed, the boys were excused to go watch television in the room next door.

"How long are you in town for?" Melissa asked, finally starting her meal.

"I fly back on Tuesday."

"What have you done so far?" Bill was pouring himself a scotch.

"We did some of the historical stuff today and went to the park." With a partially guilty look, Allie then threw me under the bus, "James wanted to see the *Make Way for Ducklings* statue." Bill gave me an odd look.

"It's a children's classic," I justified. "I teach first grade!" I blushed knowing that Bill probably didn't visit the Robert McCloskey tribute as a part of his courtship of Melissa. The sisters were entertained by my embarrassment, and out of the corner of my eye I could see them sharing a knowing glance.

After a few more childhood stories and one more scotch for Bill, we called it an evening. The boys tried a few more puzzle pieces on the wall and on the front door as Allie and I said our goodbyes. Melissa gave me an even longer hug at the front door.

"Hope to see you again soon."

Still riding the high from my success at dinner, I was brimming with confidence on the drive back to Allie's place. While I knew she and I weren't playing games, it was hard not to feel a sense of triumph as the evening drew to a close. Plus, in spending time with Melissa's family—pulling back and seeing the broader picture of Allie's life—there was nothing not to like. I could see myself coming back to the Boston suburbs for a summer barbecue or preschool graduation. Allie was quiet on the way home, and when her silhouette passed under a street light, she seemed to be smiling.

In addition to Allie's contentment, there was something else in the car: a growing, perceivable heat rising between us. Like a warm sensation at first, this unspoken mutual attraction soon became an unreachable itch begging to be scratched. I rested my forehead against the coolness of the car window, but there was only one way to douse this fire. I knew it and Allie knew it. There was an inevitability about what would happen next.

We were barely in the door, when Allie threw off her coat and kicked off her boots. Backing me against the wall, she lunged at me with a newfound desire. Our hunger for each other had never been greater, and we kissed ravenously, running our frustrated hands over each other's clothed bodies. Her lips retreated for a moment and while she exhaled deeply, her blue eyes, now filled with longing, consented as did a slow, deliberate nod of her head. Taking my hand she led me to the door of her bedroom. Opening it slowly, Allie walked me across the line she told me she didn't want us to cross. The barrier she previously established was withdrawn, as Allie decided she no longer needed to be protected by it.

CHAPTER 15

SMALL DEEDS

The sound of wind whipping through leafless branches woke me in the morning. Nestled under a fluffy down comforter, I was protected from the chill outside the window. The flannel sheets and sturdy mattress were a significant upgrade from the living room couch. The company wasn't bad either. Her feminine form laid next to me in nothing but a white vintage James Taylor concert t-shirt. I observed the simple act of her exhaling in her sleep and ever so gently traced the outline of a few stray hairs on her pillow.

I rolled over and looked at my watch; the second hand moving was a stark reminder that it was my last full day in Boston. I slipped out of the bed, got dressed quietly, and went out to the living room. The morning was still, with the exception of the clock ticking and occasional gusts of wind outside. As I sat in the charades chair, I noted the set of sheets, pillow, and homemade quilt neatly folded and stacked on one end of the couch. *Won't be needing those anymore!* I thought to myself.

When I bought the airline ticket to Boston, there was no guarantee about what would or wouldn't happen. As much as I felt for Allie, there was a chance she would not reciprocate in kind. I boarded that plane with an open and curious heart, vulnerable to the possibility of being crushed. But last night, Allie and I came together in a way our younger selves could have never imagined. I could still smell traces of her on me; the scent stirred my heart. I was replaying the events of my first trip to Allie's bedroom, when she appeared in the hallway. She had added a pair of gray sweatpants to the concert t-shirt ensemble.

"Hi." She had her arms wrapped around herself to stay warm.

"Hi."

Allie sat down on the couch next to the pillow and her mom's quilt. I watched her body as it stretched and adjusted to the chilly morning.

"What are you thinking about?" she asked me.

"Tracy McKenzie's eighth-grade graduation party."

"Wow! That's not what I thought you were going to say. I don't think I remember that."

"After our dance debacle, the thought of you even remotely liking me made me incredibly weird around you for a while."

"That, I remember." She frowned.

"So, Tracy's party became this whole fourteen-year-old couples' thing and you pushed Tammy Zamorick at me because the last thing you wanted was to hang out with me."

"Hey," Allie smiled, "Tammy really liked you."

"Well, any chance I had with Tammy was blown that night. I couldn't take my eyes off you."

"Wait. Was that the party where we turned off the lights inside to see if Bryce and Tracy were kissing in the backyard?"

"Yup. We weren't quite cool enough to be at an eighth-grade make-out party where everyone was making out. But, cool enough, to be at a party where we spied on two of our friends to see if they might be getting to second base." Allie laughed heartily. "I remember so distinctly: The movie *Fast Times* was on the TV, Danny and Stuart were arguing about the pool game they were playing, and you were eating cake with Jason Matthews." Allie dramatically winced as I brought up the name of her summer boyfriend.

"Oh, my mom hated Jason," Allie tilted her head in reflection. "She may have been right about him."

"So, I'm looking at you, horrified to see you with this fake break-dancing, mullet-wearing lacrosse player; it's the first great unrequited love of my life." Allie shot a condescending, sad face my way and bowed a few notes of air violin. "You poor soul. How ever did you survive such a heart break?"

"Well," I said as I got up and sat next to her on the couch, "Years later, I tracked the girl down in Boston and had dinner with her nephews. That really showed her." I gave Allie a ticklish poke to the ribs. She playfully retreated.

"You do realize yours wasn't the only broken heart that night?"

"What do you mean?"

"Somewhere out there, sitting on a couch, a devastated Tammy Zamorick is telling the story about how you invited her to an eighth-grade make-out party and then ignored her all night." We chuckled about it. A pillow lobbed in her direction escalated into flirtatious sparring until Allie pinned me, claiming victory with a kiss on the nose.

Although it was too cold to hold hands, the connection between us felt stronger than ever as we strolled to a coffee shop Allie thought I would like. We walked five or six blocks, Allie pointing out places that were significant to her. As she toured me through her Boston life, I wanted to do the same for her—show her my world and have it be a brighter place for her presence in it. I shivered at some particularly strong northeast air and assumed that there must be a coffee house within a block of Allie's place. It didn't matter. No amount of cold or lack of caffeine could drain the reservoir of happiness within my heart. This morning, I woke up in Allie Lockwood's bed.

I understood why Allie liked Front Street Coffee. It was bohemian, cozy, and looked like a poetry reading might spontaneously break out at any minute. The bearded barista behind the counter was effortlessly pulling off a slacker look with his thrift-store tartan and wool beanie. With a disaffected expression, he tapped the register and gave me a total for our coffees. I dropped two fives on the counter, unaware the barista was just about to extend his hand to take my money. He gave a little eye roll as he collected the bills, put out at the extra effort I had forced him to exert. Apparently, the character of "slacker barista" was not on today's call sheet of extras for our Boston-based romantic comedy. I wondered if Allie noted his subtle indignation as we sat under a shelf of clay teapots.

"What's that guy's deal?" I asked softly.

"Well," Allie offered, "You didn't hand him the money."

"What?"

"You put the money on the counter. You didn't place it in his hand." I was a little taken aback by the matter-of-fact tone in which Allie was describing this recent sequence of events. It was as if she was politely reminding me I skipped a step of some ceremonial coffee buying ritual that everyone is supposed to know.

"I'm supposed to make sure I hand money to the guy who barely acknowledged me?" I looked over at the Ethan Hawke wannabe behind the counter now buried in a beat up paperback.

"Well...yes." Allie hunched over the table closer to me. "I think it's these little things where we have an opportunity to make everyone's lives better. Even if it's making sure you hand a cashier money so they don't have to pick it up off the counter, it's like you're doing that little extra to make the world a better place." Allie smiled at me, happy to have someone to share her Small Deeds Make the World a Better Place philosophy. "Don't you think so?"

"I guess...," I said and shot a confused half smile back at Allie. The debate team captain in me wanted to go twelve rounds on the nature of humanity and ethical implications of the relative placement of currency rendered for goods and services, but this was not the time nor place. This was our last day together in Boston. We moved on to less contentious topics.

We spent the afternoon walking around the Museum of Modern Art. I was worried that I would have to come up with clever and insightful things to say, but our visit was focused on viewing and not commentary. Not once did we talk about bold lines or muddled compositions. We strolled through the grounds holding hands and appreciating all the surrounding beauty. For me, watching Allie's visceral reactions to certain pieces was better than the art itself. At the end of our tour, we sat with a bronze statue, her head resting on my shoulder. Whether half-naked in bed or fully clothed on a bench, the sensation of her body next to mine was one I wanted to hold on to forever. I let her know.

"This has been amazing. Thank you."

"For what?" She picked up her head.

"Inviting me up here, this weekend, everything."

Allie looked down as she traced a circle inside my palm. "I guess tomorrow it's back to normal, huh?"

I nodded and thought about all the possible meanings of normal: lesson plans, Glen, Sunday phone calls, Thursday night TV. The last four days had been a break from normal, and I was sad to see the clock running out on this time together. I didn't want it to end without knowing when our next time together would be.

"When do you want to come and visit exotic New Jersey?" I felt her body laugh and then her posture sagged, perhaps also noting time was fleeting.

"You said your spring break is in April?"

"Yeah, it's late this year."

"I could drive down then."

We sat for a long time with the piece of metal twisted into the shape of a forest or a serpent. I had no idea of the sculptor's intentions, but I liked sitting in front of his statue, not saying much, enjoying each other's company.

I could have taken in the forest serpent statue for hours, but my time with her was coming to an end. Allie dropped me off at Logan Airport and as soon as I entered the terminal, the euphoria of the weekend quickly faded. The spell cast over Boston was broken. I was a single traveler heading back home to an empty apartment. As tremendous and magical as the long weekend had been, it was now over. Checking the departure board, I still had plenty of time to kill before my flight. I stopped at the newsstand for a magazine and a bottle of water. Consciously, I placed a ten dollar bill in the hand of the cashier, half-heartedly wondering if it made her life just a little bit better.

CHAPTER 16

KELLY'S BIRTHDAY

The gentle pounding of surf crashed into my ears over and over. As soon as one wave receded, another would break, stretch onto the sand, and eventually withdraw back into the sea. This predictable ebb and flow was interrupted only by the occasional squawk of a seagull, navigating the cloud cover. Inhaling deeply, my nose was filled with the scent of brine and late winter. With summer months long gone, I was the only denizen on the deserted beach.

Today's date, March 12th, would have been Kelly's birthday. The date had been looming in my mind like a final exam or a tax deadline. I had no idea what to expect, only that it was going to be difficult. I didn't share the date with Shannon, and I kind of hoped Allie hadn't previously committed it to memory. Likewise, I didn't want to talk to any of my family about how hard today was; I wanted to be alone. I took a personal day not wanting to bring that pain to school with me. I left the house early with a book and Kelly's mixtape.

Most of the time, I played Kelly's mix in the order she intended it to be heard and flipped the tape over when it was finished. But today, I was wearing out one track, a version of "The Water Is Wide" by Karla Bonoff. The intentional guitar picking and wistful accordion was the right soundtrack for the trip down Route 539. With the evergreen trees of the Pine Barrens passing my car's windows, I listened to the song, rewound the tape, and played it over and over. Like waves crashing on the beach, I let the lyrics and music hit my heart again and again.

Long Beach Island (LBI) was about a two-hour drive from my apartment. There were shorter drives to the ocean, but today had to be LBI. This was where Kelly and I went last summer. Where we biked the eighteen-mile spit of land, from lighthouse to wildlife refuge and then back again. Where we had banana nut muffins from Beachbreak Cafe. So, the beach in front of Pearl Street was where I invited myself, and no one else, to Kelly's 21st birthday party.

I wasn't quite sure why, but I figured this was the place to feel closest to her. Kelly's ashes were spread into a stream on the grounds of her favorite Adirondack camp. That tributary eventually empties into the St. Lawrence River, which joins the Great Lakes, the Mississippi River, and the Atlantic Ocean. By laying her to rest in a stream, I had this silly thought that somehow Kelly was now connected to all bodies of water. (I recently taught my first graders about the water cycle, but omitted any spiritual dead sister aspects of evaporation and precipitation.) While Kelly had no gravestone, I felt anywhere there was water was a place to connect with her.

So I sat on the cold sand of Beach Haven with my book and cup of coffee, staring into the vastness of the Atlantic. I left Grief back at my apartment, but somehow he made his way here and was down the beach chucking rocks into the water. Contemplating where the ocean met the sky, I reflected upon how none of it made any sense. *Why was I sometimes filled with so much sadness, but unable to cry one tear to release any anguish? Why did Kelly waste her energy being the light of other people's lives when her own life was shaded with so much darkness? Will my life ever completely go back to being normal?*

As I ruminated with my thoughts, the sun cut through a partly cloudy sky. The image reminded me of a church bulletin cover, the kind my dad handed out to patrons as a volunteer usher back at Grace Redeemer Lutheran. When I was a kid, sitting in itchy pants at the 11am service, I always wondered why sun splitting clouds was the preferred depiction of eternity. *Did God's marketing people tell Him that since his existence was a matter of faith, this was his best advertising campaign for his product?* These were the kind of thoughts that got me into trouble with my parents at church, like the time I told my grandma she had a piece of the body of Christ stuck in between her teeth after communion.

Perhaps if my faith were stronger, I'd have been more at peace, *knowing that Kelly was "in a better place."* The whole "better place" thing always struck me as such bullshit: someone loses a loved one and you're going to console someone by informing them their relative has upgraded their existential real estate? I understood that everyone wanted to say something comforting, but there's only so many versions of "I'm sorry for your loss" I could hear.

There were a few occasions when someone had the courage to say something outside of the few socially acceptable condolences. While I was certainly closed off to most people, there were moments when someone had the right words at the right time. A high school friend, Evan, who was in medical school at the time, displayed tremendous bedside manner as we took a drive in his used Toyota Camry. It was after dark, and I needed to get away from the frantic energy of planning the funeral. On the way to a local dive bar, he offered me this wisdom.

"You know why I know you'll be okay?"

"Not really."

"Because you won't waste any energy worrying about where Kelly is now."

"What?"

"It's like when we were younger and there would be a magician at a birthday party. After every single trick, Nathan Stinson would always try to come up with an explanation of how it was done. He *had* to have an answer, even if it was the wrong one." I smirked remembering our friend Nathan, who in addition to being a bad magic explainer, was the kid who wanted to compare every single question and answer after an AP Physics test.

"You're saying it's good I don't care."

"No. I'm saying you're smart enough to realize you can't know everything. You're willing to ask questions that may not have answers. You can live with ambiguity."

Live with ambiguity. I never really considered that about myself until my chauffeur that night, our class valedictorian, suggested it.

Sure, I could be a meticulous planner who didn't like being wrong in matters of mathematics and music trivia, but I respected the limits of what could be known. There are mysteries in life, and the afterlife, I knew I couldn't unravel. Like so often in high school, Evan was right.

There was no gray area with my parents; I'm sure they thought Kelly was in heaven, floating on a cloud, wings and all. As ridiculous as that sounded to me, I was the one sitting in front of the ocean, trying to sense my sister in a substance that covers two-thirds of the earth's surface. Who's to say who was right, but I did know at a young age that organized religion was not for me. Mom and Dad sent me to Sunday school and Bible camp, but for me the best part of church was eating donuts and playing tag after the service. It might have been the itchy pants or the lengthy sermons; I was leaning toward atheism by the time I had my first deep conversation on weed in college.

My sister certainly had more room in her life for religion than I did. After my college graduation, she and I spent the summer living in our childhood house without our parents. Mom had already moved on to her new relationship while Dad had taken a new job in Connecticut. At night, we would sit on our backyard deck, look at the stars among the trees, and ponder life and sometimes the afterlife.

"I do like going to church with Mom," Kelly once told me, "There's something beautiful about the music, candlelight, and the presence—especially at Christmas."

"I get that. But what if Mom wasn't there to take you? Do you think you'll go to church in college?"

"Probably not. But we'll see."

"Do you believe?"

"I don't know. Part of me does. What about you?"

"Push comes to shove, no, but…"

"But what?"

"It can't be proven, right? I can't prove there is no god, no more than Mom can prove there is one. So, we all pick a belief and go with it. It's like golf when you're on the green putting. You're studying the swells and undulations that will push your ball one way or the other. You know what they say?"

"I have a feeling you're going to tell me."

"That your belief that you have the right read is more important than you actually having the right read. Believing is more important than knowing."

"They do, huh? Who says that?" my sister asked with a smirk.

"I don't know. Pro golfers. Religious leaders." We both laughed and leaned back in our lounge chairs, watching the light from fireflies dart about the backyard.

Those were the conversations I remember from that summer. Me, fresh from college, spewing theories and ideas I picked up in the classroom or over beers. Kelly listening discriminately and wondering if her brother learned anything over the past four years. Night after night, we sat on the deck, in various degrees of sobriety, telling stories and solving the world's problems. When Kelly and I were younger, the sorting of the three kids rarely grouped us together. Jackie and Kelly were the girls; Jackie and I were the older kids. But on the deck that summer, my younger sister and I found a connection previously undiscovered in childhood. Now, I'll never talk to her again.

A tear pooled in my right eye; it might have been sadness or too much wind coming off the water. Brushing it away, a parade of thoughts streamed through my consciousness: Kelly, the deck, driving with Evan, religion, banana nut muffins, death. I noted the tide's latest advance as the ocean continued its relentless assault on the shore. For generations, beachgoers had done exactly what I was doing: stared at the ocean and tried to make sense of it all. Damned if I would be the first to do so. There I was: a sad mourner alone on the beach, living with ambiguity.

As the Atlantic began to threaten my sneakers, I picked up my copy of *A River Runs Through It* and turned to the very last page. I read aloud Norman Maclean's words—the narrator's eulogy to his family—that in the last month had become my gospel:

Eventually, all things merge into one, and a river runs through it. The river was cut by the world's great flood and runs over rocks from the basement of time. On some of the rocks are timeless raindrops. Under the rocks are the words, and some of the words are theirs.

I am haunted by waters.

Closing my eyes, I let the sound of the surf fill my eardrums. Without invitation or prompting, the waves came time after time. After every pause, the ocean's energy would build up again, before unleashing on the land. For hours I stayed on the beach, fixed in position, unsure of where to go. The day I agonized about had arrived, and now I wanted it to be over. Like so many stages of grief, the first birthday is something you just have to go through. As far as parties go, I had attended better.

CHAPTER 17

SUPER COOL CITY

When I returned home from the beach, there was a bright red number "3" on my answering machine to greet me. I reluctantly reached for the phone and had the labored conversations with my family I had spent the day avoiding. The calls were brief, and I was relieved to complete them. Sometimes, membership in the suicide survivors club was more agonizing than comforting. I didn't mention my trip to LBI to my family or retell any memories of biking to the lighthouse. Upon completing a woefully uncomfortable dialogue with my father, I hung up the phone and stared at it for a while. After a few minutes of deliberation, I picked the phone back up and dialed a familiar 617 number.

"Today was her birthday," I announced flatly.

"Oh, James! I knew it was around this time. I'm sorry I didn't remember. How are you doing?"

"Okay…I took the day off." I recounted my day to Allie, including how I listened to a cover of an English folk song on repeat. I described in detail our trip to LBI the year before.

"Sounds like a great day and a special memory."

"Yep." I agreed, holding back some tears. We spoke for almost ninety minutes, which wasn't long enough. Today hurt. Lying in bed, staring at the ceiling, the sleeplessness matched the long nights during the time Kelly went missing. The wound was reopened. I wished for the day and the aching to be over.

If there is an upside to insomnia, it creates more hours in the day that *could* be spent productively. At 4:30am, I resigned myself to not being able to sleep, sat down at the table, and started filling in the empty time blocks of next month's lesson plans. In the creative world, pain produces great works of extraordinary creativity. Consider Pink Floyd's "Wish You Were Here" or Fleetwood Mac's "Rumors." I never wrote or recorded a platinum-certified album, but the year after my sister died, I built a city.

As a class project, Room 22 built a model of a city. The students collected an assortment of cereal boxes and other recycled items, covered them in newspaper, and painted on windows and billboards. Among the skyscrapers, we had an airport, a suspension bridge, and a water tower fashioned from a two-liter soda bottle. The kids were very proud, and rightfully so, the city was quite impressive.

We held regular "city council" meetings, and one of the first items on the agenda was to name the bustling metropolis. Given the creativity of the average six-year old, the two leading candidates were "Super City" and "Cool City." While neither were terribly impressive options, loud and opinionated factions quickly coalesced around each name. Tony Ferraro chanting "Super City" over and over was very persuasive with his peers. In the end, I taught the two camps the age-old civic strategy of compromise and thus "Super Cool City" was born.

I was discussing some city business before lunch with two council members when Sheri's head popped in my doorway.

"What brings you all the way down to this end of the school?"

"I wanted to see this cardboard city our principal is bragging about." Sheri looked over the skyline of Super Cool City with the appropriate amount of educational curiosity. "Well done, Mr. Nakamura. And the kids are having a good time with it?"

"Absolutely. You just missed a hotly contested debate on whether Lot 18 should be allocated for a roller-blade park or a movie theater."

"Are you joking?"

"Not at all." I explained to Sheri the grid system that mapped out the real estate on the floor and showed her the "building permits" I created with minimal words so even my barely literate students could initiate a project.

"In all seriousness, I'm really impressed. In addition to the social studies unit, you've got lots of reading, writing, and speaking built into this." Sheri's approval meant a lot to me. Most of the time, the faculty dismissed me as the young teacher who wanted to play kickball with the kids during recess. I wasn't widely recognized for my instructional ability. Looking around at the cluttered paint station and pile of used cardboard, I knew I was onto something. My phonic instruction of diphthongs may have needed work, but I could engage students with the best of them.

"Thanks, Sheri! I'd like to see some of the second grade teachers manage this chaos."

"Speaking of chaos, how's your love life?"

I had no idea where to begin. I said the first thing that popped into my head. "Allie's going to come down here in April." My heart skipped a beat thinking about her.

"What about Shannon?"

"She's awesome. We're having a great time hanging out."

"And she doesn't mind being on the JV team?" Sheri asked with suspicion.

"I mean we've talked about it." I explained, feeling the justification in my voice. "I was totally honest from the beginning and… she's still with Craig." Any pride I felt as a municipal planner quickly waned as the conversation suddenly felt like an interrogation.

"Do you ever hang out with Shannon's friends?"

"No…we talked about going to a basketball game with her Rutgers friends, but…"

"They went without you."

"What?"

"Shannon may be okay being your side piece, but she's not going to parade you in front of her friends and family." My thoughts immediately jumped to the dinner party in Melrose and preschool comedy with puzzle pieces. "It's pretty obvious you're in love with Allie." Sheri stopped and gestured confidently at me. "I don't think the love pentagram is a particularly stable structure. At some point, stress will break one or more of the sides."

In the midst of her geometry love lesson, Sheri was called away to mediate a dispute on the playground between two of her girls. I was taken aback by Sheri's bluntness and inferred that she thought I might not be treating Shannon fairly; until that moment, I had never truly considered that I might be doing anything wrong. *Was Shannon keeping our relationship out of sight?* With the exception of the Christmas Party, we had never spent any time with other people—we existed in a vacuum. Glancing over the suburbs of Super Cool City, I wondered about the love lives of the imaginary people living in the milk carton colonials. I bet they didn't have the long-distance bills calling Boston, which I did. They were probably happily married newlyweds who got everything they wanted from their gift registry and watched *Everybody Loves Raymond*. I hated them.

Sheri's conversation was on my mind when I had dinner with Shannon two days later. As we sat across from each other at a Chinese restaurant, I felt like we were surrounded by milk carton newlyweds. I surmised that everyone else in Peking Pavilion had their lives figured out and the two of us were merely playing grown-up. After ordering, I took a break from people watching and noticed Shannon was strangling a black cloth napkin with her hands.

"So, I have some news."

"Yeah?" I put down my green beer bottle, and she gave the poor napkin a break.

"You know I have my doubts about being a classroom teacher. While I love kids, I think I might be better off working with one at a time as opposed to standing in front of a class of thirty." Shannon paused, and I nodded. "So…I've decided to get certified in speech therapy, which as an added benefit, will require *another* degree. I've been accepted to a handful of programs, and I'm going to start in the fall." Shannon exhaled, seemingly relieved to have told me her news.

"That's wonderful. You'll be great at that. So where are you going?"

"Looks like Temple or Ohio State. Temple is close to my parents, and I have tons of high school friends in Philly. But the financial package from Ohio State is so much better."

Looking across at her, I saw Shannon's face in front of the faded wallpaper appeared as a television image, a broadcast of a high school senior with two college baseball caps on a table, one of them about to be selected. I was detached from this major decision, feeling no anxiousness about where Shannon's studies took her next. I also knew that she had already made up her mind. You don't grow up with eight brothers and sisters without healthy doses of frugality and pragmatism.

"So, it sounds like you might be leaning toward Ohio State?"

She nodded, "It's pretty hard to turn down that money." Shannon relaxed in her seat, becoming increasingly comfortable with this conversation.

"Totally." Perhaps if things were different between us, I would have been more affected. Maybe I would have made a stronger case for the program that was only an hour away. But on that day, my feelings for Shannon weren't clouding my ability to objectively see what was best for her. I hadn't considered where we'd be watching Thursday night TV when the new fall season debuted. Over that course of hot and sour soup, we were more friends than lovers. Right before the bill, Shannon had even more news.

"There was something else I wanted to tell you."

"What's that?"

"Next week, I'm going home to my parents for a few days. I'm having my appendix removed."

"Really?"

"It's not a big deal," she blushed. "The doctor wants to do it now before anything serious happens." As her face reverted to her more natural complexion, her eyes turned an even more beautiful shade of hazel. Instantly, worry crept in and I dreaded something happening to this beautiful face.

"Can I ask you a favor?"

"What?"

"When you're out of surgery, at some point can you call me and let me know you're okay?"

"Of course." Shannon flashed me that 1000-watt smile, which lit up her eyes, making them even more captivating. Taking the vision of her in, I realized how stunning my dinner companion was. I was so convinced that Allie and I were going to wind up together, but *maybe if things were different...maybe if Kelly hadn't died and Allie and I never reconnected.* Who knows? Someday, I thought, I'll figure this whole thing out. I cracked open a fortune cookie and considered the ancient Chinese wisdom printed in a Yonkers factory:

Happiness is not a destination; it's a way of life.

Fuck you, fortune cookie.

CHAPTER 18

WAITING

The roster of the New York Jets flashed across the screen as 8-bit music played a celebratory fanfare. A good chunk of the day had been spent playing the 1990 season of Tecmo Super Bowl, culminating in a championship victory over the San Francisco 49ers. I had beaten the game many times before, so this title was not particularly satisfying. Even though I ably guided one of the weakest rosters in the game to the Promised Land, as we learned from last week's fortune cookie: *Happiness is not a destination.*

A vintage classroom clock hung on the wall, a souvenir of my days working in the Bexley Library in college. The black analog numbers were thick, boring, and encased in a dingy plastic cover. A glance revealed that four minutes had passed since the last time I looked at it. I vowed to myself not to check the time for at least another fifteen minutes, a promise I broke eight minutes later. The red second hand crawled around the clock face, tormenting me with its agonizingly slow journey through the numbers.

I trudged to the kitchen and apathetically opened up the refrigerator door, confirming the contents were exactly the same as they were an hour ago. After making a mental note that I needed eggs, I picked up the phone, checked for a dial tone, and quickly put the receiver back in its cradle. Before the days of cell phones, this is what you did: checked for a dial tone to make sure your landline phone was working. Another look at the wall and three more minutes had passed: it was now 4:25 p.m. *Why hasn't she called?*

Using my detective skills, I dutifully recreated the timeline. The surgery was scheduled for 8 a.m. and it was supposed to take about an hour. The anesthesia should have absolutely worn off by now. Even if Shannon were staying in the hospital overnight, surely she was awake by now. And if she was conscious, she would absolutely remember that she was supposed to call me. The only reason for her not to call was if something had gone wrong....

Three quick, ragged breaths escaped my lungs. I closed my eyes and felt the percussion of my heart against my chest. *It's okay. It's okay; you're okay.* I reassured myself with limited success. I considered running to the grocery store for eggs and a few other staples, but I didn't want to leave the phone. Weakened by hunger and dread, I collapsed on the couch. Eyeballing the clock I saw only two more minutes had passed. *Damn!*

It was far too easy to recall the last time I had watched a clock so closely, the image of the grandfather clock at Bruce's house shelved in my memory. It was bad enough that my mom had moved in with him, but now that our childhood house had been sold, this was the closest thing to home. The standing clock stood in the living room amongst the plastic ferns and oil paintings of golf courses. As we all sat around and waited, its gold pendulum oscillated slowly, mocking me with its deliberate pace. Its absurdly loud ticking contrasted the stillness of the moment matched only the nonsensical chiming on the hour. I wanted to smash the thing to pieces with one of Bruce's prized antique golf clubs.

This was the time of waiting when Kelly was missing. One of Bruce's neighbors, Bill Trickle, organized the search party. Bill was a barrel-chested man in his sixties, whose claim to fame was that he played professional football before peddling life insurance. We spent hours tromping through woods around the golf course, which wasn't nearly as fun as playing disc golf stoned in the Alabama woods. As Bill pushed through the brush and stepped over logs, he kept reciting, "She's okay. We're going to find her." When he wasn't offering his mantra of reassurance, he was retelling football stories about the NFL in the late 1950s. Every time he opened his mouth, my brain screamed *Shut the fuck up, Bill! What if she's not okay? We may not find her!* Even back then, I had a sinking sensation that this story was not going to have a happy ending.

On day three, I left Bill's posse and I joined the vigil of family and friends back at the house. Slumped on couches or pacing the room, we alternated between suggesting optimistic possibilities and incredibly uncomfortable silences. There wasn't much to do besides try to ignore the clock and periodically check the dial tone of the kitchen phone to make sure it was working. We sat in stillness until the police knocked on the door with the worst news imaginable. *Hey! Someone tell Bill to call off his stupid search.*

I was the one who answered the front door that morning. At 7:03 two police officers, hats in hand, decided to start their day by ruining my life. As soon as I saw their faces, I knew what they were going to say; their body language and posture said it all. Numbness washed over me, and everything started moving in slow motion. Cars decelerated. The policemen froze in place. Heels clicked down the hallway. Turning my head toward the approaching pumps, I saw the figure of Susan Sutton. She read the body language of the officers as well and distress began to fill her face. Frame by frame, she collapsed to the floor as if Officer Langford had removed his revolver and shot her in the chest.

Susan was a busy bee of a person my mom knew through church. She had arrived at Bruce's house before the police did with more missing signs printed on canary-colored paper. A woman of devout faith and unbridled emotion, she was one of those people whom I questioned if they truly felt as blessed and happy as they appeared to be. Well, absolutely not this morning. Her body, unable to contain the tragedy, crumpled into a pile in the hallway. With the unexpected grace of a ballerina, her torso folded neatly onto her skirt, which fanned out in an almost perfect circle. Canary-colored fliers, which escaped Susan's grip as she fell, fluttered to the floor all around her. After four days of uncertainty, Susan's fall punctuated the truth I would now live with for the rest of my life: Kelly was dead.

Six months later, I had no idea what Officer Langford looked like or the name of everyone who was in Bruce's living room. But saved in my memory was the replay of the bright yellow fliers falling gently around the middle-aged woman lying on the tile floor. What I didn't know then was that—waiting for Shannon's call, searching for the lost mixtape, and worrying about my missing sister—were all the same version of dread. Playing Tecmo Super Bowl and monitoring the classroom clock put me right back in Bruce's living room. I couldn't escape the dark place without knowing if Shannon was okay.

In the middle of some futile breath exercises, the phone erupted from across the apartment. Adrenaline shot my weary body off the couch so I would get there before it rang a second time. Relief flooded my chest. After answering with a harried "Hello?" the voice that responded was not the one I was expecting.

"Hey! How are you?" I paused. The call was from Boston, not South Jersey.

"Hey...I'm good. What's up?"

"Just got back from shopping with my sister. She asked about you." Allie announced coyly.

"That's great." My brain was so fried. I couldn't manage the basic functions of simple conversations.

"What's going on with you? How's the city project going?" All of sudden, Greenridge, Super Cool City, and the milk carton newlyweds all seemed worlds away. I was so wrapped up in worrying about Shannon that Allie's question reminded me that there were other aspects of my life.

"Good...really good." I couldn't string a whole sentence together. Then, I realized I was tying up the phone. I was pushing Allie away, and I was tying up the phone. I was useless, and she knew it too.

"Is everything okay? You seem really distracted." *How was I supposed to answer this question?*

"Yeah?" I offered, "Actually...Allie...I'm sorry. I'm waiting for someone to call me back. Would it be okay if I called you later tonight?"

"Why didn't you just say so?" Allie's sweet voice playfully reprimanded me. "Of course. Call me back. I've got some pretty big news."

"Okay. Will do." I depressed the receiver button with my thumb and hit myself with the phone on the forehead several times. *What was I doing? Why in the world had I just rushed off the phone with Allie? Why was Shannon's status so important? Having your appendix out was not a matter of life or death,* but I had to know. This was not a time to live with ambiguity.

If Shannon wasn't going to call me, I'd have to call her. Not having her parents' number would be a challenge. But there was a time when entire jobs were dedicated to helping people find other people's phone numbers. You could call directory assistance, provide a city and a surname, and they'd promptly supply you with the number you were seeking. It wasn't the days of female operators connecting actual phone cords, but the concept was the same.

Closing my eyes and waving the phone receiver like a magic wand, I attempted to conjure up Shannon's home town and father's name. Since "Walsh" was a pretty common last name there might be multiple Walsh entries in...*which city? Where did she go to high school? It's near Cherry Hill.* Ultimately, the memory tumblers clicked into place and I got the combination I needed: *Patrick Walsh in Collinswood, NJ.*

A nasally voice gave me the digits I needed, and I cautiously rang the Walsh household. I felt foolish. I felt silly checking on her after a routine surgery, but I had to know. As I waited through four rings, my heart thumped. I prayed that she would answer, but I got a man's voice instead.

"Hello."

"Hi. My name is James Nakamura. I was calling for Shannon, please." I grimaced at my over-the-top politeness. The "please" was a little too much.

"She's not available right now. Can I take a message?" The voice was stern and authoritative.

"Oh… okay. I'm a friend of hers from…. Uh…I'm a friend of hers from…school. I was just calling to make sure she came out of surgery okay."

"Yes, she's okay. She's resting. I'll let her know you called." Before I could respond, the stern voice was gone. My right ear was filled with the echo of the dial tone. Any relief I felt couldn't overcome the ambient stress I had felt all day. As it turns out I had nothing to worry about; my phone was just fine…so was Shannon.

CHAPTER 19

TWO PHONE CALLS

Shannon called and apologized the next day.

"I was pretty out of it," she explained.

"It's okay. I started to get a little worried because I hadn't heard from you." I felt guilty accepting an apology when perhaps I should have been offering one. Not that I had wronged anyone, but I wasn't exactly proud of my previous day's behavior. While Shannon couldn't see me cringe thinking about yesterday's waiting and worrying, she did make sure I remembered my phone call.

"So... you tracked down my parents' phone number?" she inquired with a healthy dose of levity and feigned moral superiority. "What are you—some kind of stalker?"

"I know..." I said. "I'm sorry if it was weird to call your house."

"I'm just kidding with you," she laughed. "For a second, I wasn't sure it was you. All my father said was that some Japanese guy called."

"I didn't have the chance to tell him that my mother is Dutch English, but I'm glad you were able to figure it out."

"At first, when he told me I got a phone call, I thought he was talking about Craig, but…" Her words trailed off. I waited—not knowing what to say. "I…I haven't spoken to Craig for a couple of months."

"Really?" I responded with too much excitement.

"Yep."

"I had no idea." I pounded my hand into my forehead. *Like it was my job to keep track of Shannon's communication with her boyfriend/ex-boyfriend?* As stupid as I felt, I was also dumbfounded. *Shannon had been single for months and didn't let me know.*

"Well…I didn't tell you because I wasn't exactly sure what it meant for us."

For us. Shannon had referred to her and me as "us." While I understood the pronoun, I hadn't really considered that we were an "us." She may not have even been suggesting that we were an "us," but the way she said it struck me.

"You want to know something funny?" she asked. "It was the last thing I thought about before my surgery. There I was in a hospital gown, inhaling gas. I was at that point where you feel yourself going under and you sort of fight it. And you know what idea keeps crossing my mind? I gotta tell James I'm not with Craig anymore."

"Moment of clarity?" I said, sort of joking.

"I guess so," Shannon answered thoughtfully, which made me feel guilty about my flippant response to her anesthesia story. The line was silent before she continued. "It's weird because we never officially broke up, never had the big, loud 'I never want to see you again' argument. We slowly faded out of each other's lives. Tell you the truth, I wish we had the big breakup argument." More silence. "A few weeks ago, I was doing laundry and I saw some of his t-shirts at the bottom of my drawer and I'm like 'What am I holding on to these for?' That afternoon I donated his t-shirts along with some other old clothes. Craig had no idea, but our relationship came to an end at a Goodwill store on Livingston Avenue."

My god, Sheri was right. Suddenly, one of the points of the love pentagram was gone, leaving the rest of us configured in a love trapezoid or love parallelogram. More importantly, *what was Shannon telling me and why was she telling me it? Was she about to tell me that through her surgical experience it dawned on her that she could no longer participate in whatever it was we were participating in?*

"I'm really glad you told me." Coming out of my mouth, it sounded like something a counselor would say to a support group, but it was true. Then I added something I felt like my mom would have said, "I hope you know you could have told me this sooner."

"I guess I didn't tell you because I didn't want you to add any expectations to what we were doing because my situation had changed."

"Expectations?" I was going into full-on therapist mode.

"When we…when we started, it was clear you and I were both… with other people. You and I never had the exclusive conversation, and I didn't want to assume we were. So I had this realization about Craig, I didn't want to put any additional pressure on you, especially with everything that you've been through."

Ouch. *Everything I've been through.* Shannon is treating me with kid gloves in the love trapezoid because my sister killed herself. *Who needs a therapist now?* Her intentions may have been good, but her words landed somewhere between thoughtful and condescending. I took a step back from having my feelings hurt and attempted to help make sense of it.

"Forget about me for a second. You're entitled to want what you want." *Want what you want? That's real fucking brilliant, James.*

"I don't know. I like what we have," Shannon contemplated. "So much of my life seems like it's one big transition: Craig, graduation, student teaching, and now grad school. This is going to sound horrible, and please don't take this the wrong way, but spending time with you has been such a welcomed diversion from all it. I'm okay not asking any big questions about us if you're okay with it."

There was that word again: us. A variety of thoughts competed for my attention. Part of me was happy Craig was no longer in the picture; I had outlasted him in the Shannon Sweepstakes. *At the same time, if Craig was no longer a consideration, wouldn't she want a full-blown relationship with me? Or was she merely protecting herself? What if she had wanted the complete and comprehensive James boyfriend experience? With Allie in the picture, was that option even on the table?*

"I'm okay with not asking big questions." *James, you big fucking liar. That's all you do is ask big questions.* I imagined it was true and tried to chart a reasonable path forward. "What if we get to a point where this doesn't work for one of us, we've got to let the other person know." *Now I was using the word us.* "You'll tell me if you get to that point?"

"Of course I will." Even though we had no eye contact, I could tell she was smiling as she said that. "You, too?

"Well, typically I like women who still have their appendix intact, but for you, I'll make an exception."

"Shut up. Don't make me laugh; it makes my side hurt."

"In all seriousness, I'll let you know." We had conversations like this before, but this one was by far the most explicit. What started after bagels and an acknowledgment of other romantic interests, was now feeling a little less casual. This was the most relationship-y talk we had ever had. With the post-appendectomy accord in place, we moved on to the easier discussions of Shannon's health.

"So how are you feeling?"

"Tender. I'm moving pretty slowly, but I'm doing okay."

"How long are you going to be at your parents' house?"

"Like another week."

"Do you want me to come down and see you?"

"You don't have to do that."

"I know. I want to."

"Let me see how I'm doing in a couple days. I'd like to be able to get up to answer the door."

"You might have to because I'm not sure your dad is too keen on letting half-Japanese guys into his house."

"You're the worst," Shannon held in a laugh. The joking was a nice contrast to the serious tone of the earlier part of the conversation. After some more small talk, Shannon had to go; her mom was reminding her it was time to take her pain medication.

I gently hung up the phone and painted a picture in my head of Shannon lying on a plaid couch, recuperating in comfy sweatpants. Perhaps her parents' living room was draped in wood paneling and adorned with pictures of all the kids in soccer uniforms and graduation gowns. Maybe her mom was busy doting on the patient while her dad, pretending not to be concerned, hid behind a Robert Ludlum book in his recliner. A *Cheers* rerun was on in the background when Shannon laughed, though compromised by the pain in her side, her smile still lit up the room. I had no idea if my recreation of the Walsh household was accurate, but I wanted to insert myself in the scene, charm her parents, and take Shannon out for ice cream.

My hand was still on the receiver when it rang to life with another call. The vibrations startled me and shook me from my South Jersey suburban daydream. I could tell it was her. There was half a breath—a brief pause in preparation for the conversation—that was instantly identifiable. Before I had a chance to say "hello," I could feel Allie's presence through the phone line. It made me smile knowing I could picture her sitting in the "charades" chair, hair falling over one shoulder. But there was something else too, the faintest of distress signals being broadcast from Boston. Barely detectable, my sixth sense picked up something in the microsecond of air time to start the call. Before I could even properly greet her, she dropped the bomb.

"Glen and I broke up."

CHAPTER 20

CLOSER TO FREE

A jolt of the car brakes buckled my head backward. I remorsefully offered up my left hand to the morning commuter, letting him know I was at fault in not waiting my turn at the four-way stop at Thornton Road. While watching his car make a sweeping left turn, my fingers tapped restlessly on the steering wheel to an absent rhythm. For the first time in a long time, Kelly's mixtape wasn't playing in the car. This morning, there was no room in my brain for music. In a series of phone calls, Shannon, and then Allie, had both announced that their previously existing relationships were no longer existing. I had thought of nothing else since.

Once in my classroom, I lackadaisically went through my morning routine. I nearly stapled myself assembling more journals and got marker on my shirt as I was writing the day's sight words on the easel. Sitting down on a chair made for a much smaller human, I contemplated what originally were two flings with two women. *This was supposed to be consequence-free fun, part of the universe's plan to pay me back for the awfulness of the year before.* Wasn't the pentagram supposed to afford me ease and freedom? After too long of a stretch of thinking, I determined another cup of coffee was the solution.

As I started the long trek down the corridor to the faculty room, music started running through my head. By the time I reached the custodian's office, I was absentmindedly singing loudly enough for those in earshot to hear, "Everybody wants to live how they wanna live and everybody wants to love how they want to love." As I belted out the theme song from *Party of Five,* unbeknownst to me, someone was listening to my solo. Turning the corner I continued singing "Everybody wants to be…" and was immediately surprised to make contact with a familiar sixth grade face who joined in to finish the verse.

"Closer to freeeeeeee," we sang to each other. My duet partner turned out to be Megan Landry, who was captain of the safety patrol. Megan was a self-aware goofy girl with braces, but popular enough to have the top spot of the sixth graders who helped maintain "law and order" in the hallways. She was putting on her bright orange captain sash when she caught me mid-song.

"Nice one," I complimented her.

"Mr. Nakamura!" she exclaimed, "You watch *Party of Five?*"

"Of course."

"Oh my God! I love Bailey!" she proclaimed throwing her wiry arms up in the air. And her enthusiasm summoned a few of her friends over to our conversation. Whether it was knowledge of pop culture or the fact that I was decades younger than most teachers at

Greenridge, I had a fair amount of street credibility with the sixth graders. Before I knew it, I was in conversation with two of Megan's friends, Clarissa and Samantha, discussing Bailey's love possibilities at Grant High School. When we ran out of plot lines to discuss, Samantha checked in on my relationship status.

"Mr. N, are you married?"

"Of course not," Clarissa corrected. "He doesn't have a ring on." The proud girl said it with all the certainty of the student who won this year's spelling bee. I appreciated the absoluteness with which Clarissa operated. In her world anyone who's married would have to have a ring on. If only love and relationships could be determined so easily.

"Do you have a girlfriend?" Samantha persisted. For several reasons, I wasn't sure how to answer, and before I could, Megan weighed in on the subject.

"I heard that Mr. Nakamura was dating Mrs. Gale's student teacher," looking at her two friends and telling them as if I wasn't there. I took this as my cue to continue on with my coffee quest.

"Rumors, gang, just rumors." I advised and turned and walked away, shielding a smile from the safety patrol leadership. By now, I was well-accustomed to questions about my personal life and fashion critiques from eleven-year-olds. Like the sympathy cards my class had made for me last fall, their honesty was inevitable. In my experience, children's pure unfiltered reactions had a way of voicing the truth, without any pretense of how it should be told. These girls were still a couple years away from playing serious games in matters of social status and romance, and their untarnished and naive transparency was one of the things I loved about elementary school.

Entering the faculty room, I considered Samantha's "Do you have a girlfriend?" question. *How would I answer that question honestly?* Sure I was older, wiser, and more mature than the sixth grade population, but wasn't I also much better at lying to myself? To this point, I had been so self-congratulatory for being honest with Allie and Shannon, *what version of the truth was I telling James?* Wouldn't it be nice to live in Clarissa's world where the presence of a ring meant true love and real commitment?

The *Party of Five* conversation was a welcome diversion and gave me confidence that I would be able to compartmentalize my life once my students arrived. But until then, I was going to dwell on the conversation I had with Allie the night before. As I grabbed my mug off the wooden peg board next to the refrigerator, it replayed in my head on repeat. Time and time again, I heard her sweet voice announce "Glen and I broke up" with equal parts pain and possibility.

"What happened?"

"He wanted a bigger commitment…said he wanted to take the next step. He suggested that we move in together and based on my reaction to that, he got really upset."

"Allie, I'm really sorry." Seemed like the right thing to say.

"When he calmed down, we talked about what really was going on between us. In addition to…other developments…we had some of our own issues. At times, he wasn't supportive of my career; he said I would disappear for stretches. I won't bore you with all the details. Ultimately, we determined that we want different things."

"So what do you want?" I blurted out. I couldn't help myself. Predicting her response, I assumed this was the part where she would say she wanted me.

"I'm not sure." *Wrong answer,* but she went on, "Right now, it hurts and it's confusing."

"I get that." In reality, I *didn't* get what was confusing, but I was trying to practice a degree of empathy. While I was internally performing a victorious tap dance, I wanted to maintain a sympathetic ear. She was crying, not sobbing, but mourning the end of a relationship. There were long pauses interrupted by her ragging breathing and tears escaping. Toward the end of our conversation, she composed herself.

"James?'

"Yeah."

"I get this must be a lot to drop all of this on you. I want you to know, throughout this whole thing, I've been thinking a lot about you as well." The tone of her voice changed and became more self-assured. I had no idea what she was going to say next. I was hanging on every word. *Was she about to proclaim her love for me? Is this where we start planning our lives together?* "I...I'm not 100% sure what this means for you and I. Just because this is over, doesn't mean I can jump in with both feet with you. Part of me wants to, but I need to see what you and I are without being in the shadow of me and Glen."

The shadow of me and Glen certainly wasn't the warm, fuzzy response I was looking for. So many times I had envisioned the moment when Allie would tell me she was no longer hindered by another relationship; I assumed it would be more like a Fourth of

July parade and less like a funeral procession. I expected her to run to me and leap into my arms instead of tears and cautious evaluation.

"So what does that mean?"

A deep exhale left Allie's soul. "It means, right now, I can't tell you what you probably want to hear. I know you want more—can feel how much you want more—but, at this moment, I'm not there." My heart sank to a depth I didn't know it could access.

"Okay...," I replied hoping for a softer landing.

"But, it also means I am really excited to come see you in a couple weeks. I want to see where your life is and be a part of it. Every time we've been together, since...you know, it's been amazing. Nothing has changed that." Her voice was light and determined, the exact opposite of how the call started.

"Me too. But I have to ask, when will I know..."

"If I'm on board?" She finished my thought.

"Well...yeah." It was my turn to take a deep breath. "It's like we're at some lake house up in the Adirondacks. I'm in a canoe, holding two paddles, waiting for you. You're on the dock deciding if you're going to get in the boat or not. I can't row across the lake without you. I thought...."

"You thought without Glen I'd be ready."

"I did."

"Well, this is where I am right now. In less than two weeks, I am planning to be there. Are you still willing to have me come down if I'm still unsure?"

"Of course."

"Then I'll see you in ten days."

"Ten days."

I was so lost in the previous night's conversation I didn't notice one of the secretaries patiently waiting for her caffeine fix. Obliviously parked right in front of the coffee machine, I apologized and sat down on one of the blue couches with my "world's greatest teacher" mug. Outside the window, the first round of buses pulled into the parking lot. Thank god for soon-to-be-arriving needy first graders that would occupy my time and pull my attention back to the present. Bring on the distractions of finding lost lunch money and securing untied shoelaces, anything to stop overthinking about last night. As for the future, Allie would be here in ten days—make that nine days. *By that time, she'd come around and realize she's in love with me, right?* I took a sip of weak faculty room coffee and told myself I was strong enough to make it.

CHAPTER 21

LAMBERTVILLE

Allie Lockwood was actually standing in the middle in my living room. I wanted to reach out and poke her in the arm to make sure she wasn't a figment of my imagination. But both her dirty green hatchback parked outside my window and her suitcase propped up against my couch were real enough. It looked like she brought enough clothes for the three days we had planned, and I already wished she was staying longer. Grief was nowhere to be found; I told him to get lost for the weekend. I stole another embrace, losing myself in her blonde hair and the soft, lingering scent of her conditioner. My one-bedroom apartment, which has been the setting of much of my nightmare, now felt like a dream.

Allie rewrapped her ponytail and scanned my mostly blank walls with a degree of discernment.

"Can I ask you a question?"

"Of course," I said, handing her a bottle of water.

"Why does every guy's apartment look like he just moved in or is about to move out?" she submitted with a smile. I took a look at my spartan furnishings and decor, concluding that it did have a certain extended-stay hotel aesthetic.

"Not everybody can be a professional painter," I said, joining her on the couch. "Besides, my decorator is on vacation."

"Sure," continuing her gentle ribbing, "but why don't you have anything hanging on the walls? It doesn't really look like a home." Apparently, my big classroom wall clock and neon dartboard weren't sufficient interior design elements in the artist's eyes.

"I don't know. I don't want to go get some art just for the sake of hanging it on the wall. If I'm going to put something up, it would be nice to mean something."

"For it to be personal?"

"Exactly."

Allie nodded and started rifling through my CDs, occasionally commenting on an artist or song. When she reached my modest library of books, she found a photo album and started browsing through it. Allie hadn't seen my sister in a while and was struck by the images of Kelly in high school and beyond. I told her more about the summer after college and sitting on our deck looking at the stars. Allie was the perfect audience, and I liked telling her about my sister, about that time. Her smile gave me permission to feel good about Kelly, something I needed to remember. When there were no more stories to tell, Allie looked around and stretched out her arms.

"So you've got me here. What are we going to do?"

"Since my luxurious apartment may not be up to your standards," I jokingly gestured, "I figured we'd go out to the Delaware River. I made a hotel reservation in Lambertville. It's about an hour away."

"Aren't you the little travel agent?" she remarked and leaned back. I could tell she was impressed.

"Gotta have something to fall back on in case this teaching thing doesn't work out."

"So what's the Delaware River like?"

"It's actually very pretty, quite scenic."

"Really?"

"Yes."

I completely understood the reason for the skepticism in Allie's voice. New Jersey is the butt of many jokes and in some cases, deservingly so. Most people wouldn't consider "the Garden State" particularly scenic, but in my time there I had found pockets and places which were absolutely beautiful. One of them was the Delaware River Gap, particularly in springtime. When the trees are full of sparrows and the riverbanks are painted with wildflowers, it's the quintessential picture of hope and renewal.

Dotted along both sides of the Delaware River were quaint little New Jersey and Pennsylvania hamlets. They were mostly untouched by corporate globalization and retained their unique charm. Their streets were full of local merchants who later would be threatened by e-commerce, but in the mid-90s no one was logging onto Amazon to buy wind chimes and artisan soap. Burgers were served at bars and taverns, not fast food joints, and there wasn't a cup of coffee from

Seattle to be found anywhere. Most of what Allie had seen in New Jersey had been from the Turnpike; this scenery would be an upgrade.

We arrived in Lambertville in the afternoon and strolled along the sidewalk, occasionally ducking into one of the shops if something caught our eye. Among the mom-and-pop restaurants, Main Street was populated with art galleries, antique furniture stores, and vintage clothing boutiques. Allie bought a floppy hat and wore it for the rest of the day to protect her fair skin. It coordinated well with her floral dress and like the colorful banks of the Delaware; she was the very image of springtime. At times, when her window browsing led her to a store ahead of me, the sight of her was almost too much for me to handle. Her beauty made me weak in the knees. We had dinner at a cute street-side cafe as it was warm enough to eat outside. Allie charmed the waiter; it was nice to see that she had brought some of that Boston magic to New Jersey with her.

I swirled my glass of wine. She tilted her head and asked me what I was thinking.

"I can't believe you're here."

"Why is that?"

"I don't know. Somehow seeing you in Boston was like a dream. But now that you're here—where I live—the thought of you and me together, somehow it's more real." She smiled without her teeth revealing her dimples. She put her hand on the table asking for my hand to join hers.

"I'm really happy to be here with you."

"Me too."

More dimples.

After dinner, we meandered back to the Holcombe House Inn, where we were staying for the night. The square brick building dating back to the Revolutionary War was named after some old guy who sold thimbles and needle cases to support the Continental Army. We sat in the rocking chairs on the wrap-around patio and played backgammon while crickets bounced sound off the riverbank. When we retired to our second-story room, I caught myself smirking at the "naughtiness" of staying in a hotel with Allie Lockwood. It brought back memories of the eighth-grade class trip to D.C. when I didn't have the guts to sneak up to the girls hotel floor for Skittles and spin the bottle. But on this night, I had plenty of courage, and I went everywhere I wanted to go.

After a morning of more courage and a late breakfast, we opted to rent bikes and ride the towpath, a compacted dirt trail utilized by mules to draw barges in the 1800s. I'm guessing the mules typically didn't appreciate the trees surrounding the canal, but I found pedaling through the spring greenery both serene and energizing. As we rode by wooden fences and under bridges propped up by stone abutments, it felt like one of the Saturday adventures of my childhood. We took a break just past Lock 19 to sit in the grass and watch the sun dance through the water. After a few moments of contemplative silence, she could tell that I was lost in something deep.

"What are you thinking about?"

"Water."

"Water?"

"Since my family deposited Kelly's ashes in an Adirondack stream, water—and particularly rivers—makes me feel close to her."

"How so?"

"This might sound silly, but part of me thinks that Kelly's in the water," I explained to Allie that without a gravestone to visit, anywhere near a body of water could be a cemetery. I quoted the last lines of *A River Runs Through It*, which I had committed to memory. As I explained my personal pull toward the river, Allie's brow furrowed. I thought she would appreciate my sharing of this, that this might bring us closer, but the dissidence on her face said otherwise.

"Oh…"

"Oh, what?"

"Nothing." Allie shifted her legs and averted her eyes.

"No really; what are you thinking?" I looked at her face trying to create eye contact. She gazed off into the distance.

"Well…I hear you…but that's not…true…" Allie's slow and deliberate word choice made me nervous.

"Allie, what are you talking about?"

"I believe, I know in my heart, that Kelly is in heaven." *Oh brother. We're going to have this conversation.* While Allie had a right to her faith, at the moment it was conflicting with how I was coping with my tragedy, less than a year after my sister died. Unintentionally, she was poking at the scab that was trying to heal over that wound. My eyelids closed, and my breathing became uneven.

"I know we have different beliefs," I stated the obvious with very measured speech. "I'm trying to tell you what I'm going through."

"That's fine, it's just…."

"Just what?"

"You're wrong." She finally made eye contact with me to empha-size that I had an imperfect understanding of the afterlife. I was shocked at her bluntness and her calmness made me even angrier. It didn't bother me that she wanted to be Catholic, but I couldn't comprehend her inability to give me space for my grief and what I was going through. This wasn't some sweet old lady telling me "She's in a better place" at Kelly's funeral. Allie was supposed to be my soulmate.

"Allie—you're an artist. How can your belief system be so limited?"

"Limited?" Her eyebrows were now raised. That may not have been the right word choice. What I didn't know at the time was that as much as she was disrespecting my grief, I was trampling on her religion. I didn't want to have to illustrate the absurdity of halos, wings, harps, and clouds. *How did I miss that religion was so central to her? Had I cherry-picked the parts of Allie I wanted to see at the expense of missing others. Even if I had, Allie was smart enough to allow for alternative perspectives.* Arms were crossed. The rift was getting wider.

"How do you reconcile being with me when I don't believe in heaven?"

She pursed her lips before laying this beauty on me, "Honest-ly…I feel sorry for you."

Jackpot! Allie had just hit the mother lode of all my emotional triggers. While jokes about my height, and criticizing Syracuse Bas-ketball were known to push my buttons, being pitied far surpassed being short or having to defend Coach Boeheim's postseason record.

I was livid. I couldn't believe this was the person I was in love with, the woman I had thoughts of spending the rest of my life with. The sweet "girl next door" was gone and replaced with cold, calculating Catholicism. Allie, who had been my lighthouse through this treacherous stretch, was now going dark and saying you deal with those rocks. *Feel sorry for me? Is that what this has been—a pity party since the funeral?*

"So, what? You're some sort of missionary? You're here to convert me?" The words escaped my mouth in between my angry breathing. Allie, by contrast, was as still as the surface of the canal.

"No. That's your choice if you don't want to believe." She sounded like a patronizing preschool teacher trying to reason with a four-year old throwing crayons on the floor. I was mad at Allie, and I was mad at myself. It was my fault for advancing our hypothetical relationship without doing some spiritual due diligence. In the game of Life, I was in such a rush to put Allie's pink peg in my car and drive her to Millionaire Estates that I skipped over the compatible religion space. My heart ached, and I was out of spiritual arguments.

"What are we doing?" That was my olive branch.

"You're obviously very upset." More preschool talk. "I don't know why you're so angry."

"I'm angry because I think I love you, and all I've thought about is being with you. But the person I want to spend the rest of my life with is going to pity me the whole time because my soul isn't going to heaven." My words bombarded Allie like cannonballs while she silently picked at the grass with Zen-like concentration. Sorry, with *Catholic-like* concentration. Finally, I had to ask. "What are you thinking?"

"I'm just wondering what Kelly would think?"

Oh my god! *Fuck you, Allie.* You don't get to wonder what my dead sister would think. I don't care what you think your relationship with Kelly was; leave her out of your eternal life.

It was at that moment that I knew it was over. Somehow, my concept of Allie was a mirage. I had constructed a world in my mind in which Allie was my salvation. But as it turns out, I couldn't be saved because I didn't believe in the right God. Allie knew it, too. Maybe she realized that I was holding on too tightly, that I was asking too much. But sitting next to each other next to Lock 19, we came to the same conclusion.

Our ride back to Big Al's Bike Rentals was deafly silent as was the car ride to my apartment. When we pulled into my parking lot, Allie announced she was leaving early and I didn't object. After packing her car, she dismissively handed me a piece of paper, not unlike a customer carelessly dropping dollar bills on a cashier's counter.

"What's this?"

"I drew this for you," she said spitefully and turned her back to me. Her pink peg was out of my car; she got into her Honda Civic and drove away. I stood there stunned, like what had just happened was an out-of-body experience. When Allie was closer to the 8A Turnpike entrance, I finally looked at the paper in my right hand. It was a rough sketch of charcoal on parchment. While abstract, it was clearly two figures—Allie and I—in a canoe with the mountains in the background. I closed my eyes and swallowed. Allie was no longer in my living room. Allie was no longer in my life. I looked over to the couch and saw an all too familiar figure.

I know, Grief, I'm an asshole.

CHAPTER 22

PENTAGRAM NO MORE

I never saw Allie Lockwood again. Ever since the day of debating Catholicism, we haven't spoken another word to each other. In subsequent years, I've googled her name now and then, perhaps curious about the unrealized potential of what could have been. When I did so, it looked like painting was paying the bills, and that made me happy for my eighth-grade friend. But in that time, neither of us picked up the phone or a fountain pen; both of us apparently in agreement that there was nothing left to be said or written.

In the days following The Battle of Lambertville, I was surprised at how little it affected me. As invested as I had been a few weeks earlier, in my mind the split was logical and absolute. It was probably the only time in my romantic life my head was able to out-maneuver my heart. I could now see that indulging in visions of a shared future with Allie was like injecting my soul with opium. For months, I had been hooked on these euphoric rushes that not only felt amazing, but also provided temporary pain relief. Perhaps on that bike ride, I experienced a moment of clarity which enabled me to quit cold turkey.

As furious as I was that afternoon, it wasn't Allie's fault that I overdosed on the idea of her. She was a good friend for coming to Kelly's funeral, and seeing her in the gym meant the world to me that night. What happened next was a product of grief, nostalgia, and flirtations dating back to sixth grade. Our fling kept me warm through a very cold winter and got me through some hard stretches of checking expiration dates on milk cartons. Years later, when I think back on our time together the memories, like her phone voice on a Sunday night, are sweet and endearing.

With my long-distance commitment to Boston drastically reduced, my thoughts turned to Shannon. One morning, as I packed a lunch, I caught myself comparing one woman to the other. What happened on the towpath bike ride was a referendum on Allie—an open and shut case of incompatibility, *right?* It wasn't like: "Hey, Allie. There's this other woman, and I like her better." *Or was it?* I wasn't thinking of Shannon during that argument, but *was she possibly on my mind more than I considered?* While I was fawning over my childhood crush, had a seed of another relationship germinated and began crowding out another?

Time with Allie—the gym, the bridge, Boston—had this magical quality about it. It was an all-consuming feeling of living in a story-book romance, where everything else in life, but her, slipped away. And since our relationship wasn't grounded in reality, its flames couldn't be fanned by the monotony of the everyday world. Even without the challenges we unearthed on the towpath, we couldn't stay in our dream world of smiling strangers and chocolate croissants forever.

Shannon was different. We met at work. She'd come over to watch TV on Thursdays and occasionally brought a load of laundry to preserve her stash of quarters in her dorm room. It's hard to get more grounded in day-to-day reality than rationing loose change. I poured a cup of coffee and recalled a conversation about childhood breakfast cereals. It was the morning after she stayed over for the first time, and laughing about Fruit Loops was a comforting contrast to the unfamiliarity of a new bed partner. Grabbing my car keys, I caught myself actually feeling happy. Shannon made me happy. The question now was: did she want that gig full time?

This was the topic of discussion with Sheri when our classes met for buddy story time. Inside the library, pairs of students—one fourth-grader and one first-grader—each found a nook and book for the older to read aloud to the younger. As Sheri was reading the tea leaves of my love life, you could say the teachers—one older, one younger—were paired up as well. We stood in the corner, a safe distance away from little impressionable ears. Sometimes teachers have personal conversations with their classes present; there's not enough adult time in school for anything else. Students had no idea of the soap operas to which they were sitting courtside. Sheri listened intently, all while we both kept one eye on shared reading time.

"Well, young James," she said, patting me on the back, "Your life is nothing if not entertaining." Her tone was light-hearted, and I didn't take it in a condescending way. Behind the joke, there was genuine care and concern in her voice. "Not one phone call since she left?"

"Nope."

"Wow. I gotta say; I did not see that coming. Granted I've met Shannon in person, but the way you spoke and carried on about Allie, my god, I thought for sure that you were going to wind up with her."

"I did too," I agreed but felt no regret. Still, there was a tinge of wistfulness in my response. Sheri walked over to course correct some boys who were throwing bookmarks at each other before re-examining my situation.

"You're okay with how it happened?"

"I mean, it wasn't great at the time, but I think it was inevitable."

"Inevitability," Sheri nodded. "I think my ex's attorney used that word to justify his affair. Inevitability doesn't help my kids when he's late with child support." Her bitter retort was a little out of left field, but a good reminder that Sheri had the life experience to be a fair arbiter of love. Fortunately, she chose to speak next, as I wasn't ready to weigh in on her life.

"What does Shannon think of all this?"

"I haven't told her yet. I'm seeing her tonight."

"Just be fair with her," she warned through the top of her glasses. And like her earlier jokes, her warning was also laced with pseudo-motherly concern.

Even though it was walking distance to campus, The Rail Stop was a mature enough bar that I didn't feel like a senior citizen among its clientele. The worn-down upholstery and absence of super sweet cocktails catered more to the grad school crowd. It wasn't uncommon to see doctorate candidates pounding out their dissertation with a Triumph IPA sitting next to their laptop. Shannon and I grabbed a corner booth while a long-haired band in leather jackets set up their sound equipment. After half a beer, I summoned the courage to tell her my truth.

"So Allie and I…," I paused and wasn't sure what to say. Shannon locked eyes on me. *Did we break up? Were we ever together?* "Allie and I aren't doing whatever Allie and I were doing."

"You broke up?" I nodded back to her. She glanced away, considering this new information before looking back at me. "Are you okay?" It seemed like an odd question, but Shannon was generally concerned. It was her nature to worry for others.

"I really am," I stated in complete honesty. "Have you ever had a conversation with someone and instantly you both realized it was not meant to be?" Shannon brought a finger to her lips, tilted her head, and considered the possibility.

"I don't think I have. What's it like?"

I didn't want to get into all the details, but I gave her the short version of my water spirituality, the opposing Catholic Counterpoints, and the watershed moment by the canal. Saying it out aloud felt like an admission of guilt. I also felt silly that I had lost myself in this fantasy of Allie. Shannon made it easy on me.

"I think that's beautiful that you're trying to be close to your sister." Shannon put an arm on mine as she looked at me with her big olive eyes. "You don't talk about your sister a lot." She was right. I hadn't told Shannon much of anything about Kelly. Allie had been my emotional receptacle for the last six months. Perhaps that would change.

"I think you two would have gotten along." For the first time I considered the potential, but now impossible Kelly–Shannon dynamic. "It's funny; she hated this one girl I dated right after college. Told everyone how Tara was mean to me. She didn't tell me, though, and I wish she had. Would have saved me a lot of trouble. She was right about that one."

"Did your sister know Allie?"

"Oh yeah. There was a stretch where Allie was like a second big sister to Kelly. They both loved art and spent hours drawing and sketching."

Shannon's plump lips pouted toward her beer. "It sounds like Allie was pretty important to both you and your sister," she stated flatly.

"Well," I said, "That ship has sailed." *Or*, I thought to myself, *that boat has ventured out with only one paddle.*

My last comment hung in the air for a while, and the two of us worked our beers. I assumed that the *End of Allie & James* conversation would lead into a *Beginning of Shannon & James* conversation, but neither of us ventured into those waters. So I tried another approach.

"What are you doing this weekend?"

"I've got to do some car shopping. There's no way the old mom-mobile is going to make it back and forth to Columbus. Then I'm checking out a couple places for my sister's bachelorette party."

"Do you want help with that?"

"With which one?" She looked at me quizzically.

"Either. Both. I'm a pretty good negotiator and decent party planner." Shannon continued to look at me like I was some sort of geometry proof she couldn't figure out. I made a joke to relieve some of my uneasiness, "Hey, if you don't want my help, there's probably lots of ex-student teachers that are buying cars this weekend."

"Well…you just broke up with Allie, and now you want to jump into boyfriend duty with me." Her words cut right through me. I wasn't ready for this attack.

"No…." I objected before modifying my answer, "Yes. Maybe. I don't know. What do you want?" The *Beginning of Shannon & James* conversation was not off to the greatest start.

"I want…I want us to be honest. A few months ago you wanted both of us and for a variety of reasons that worked out for everyone involved. But now there's no Allie, and I don't want to be…" Her eyes searched the bar for an answer.

"Some sort of consolation prize?" I suggested.

"Yeah…something like that."

"Hey! I'm sorry. I really haven't processed this fully," I felt guilty for joking earlier. "What I do know is Allie and I are over. She and I very clearly decided this is no-go exercise. I also know I'm here with you for a reason. The day of your surgery I was really worried about you. Granted, some of that was my own baggage, but I really felt for you that day. I still do."

With tears welling in her olive eyes, she leaned over and gave me a kiss on the cheek. It couldn't have been my incoherent ramblings; I think for whatever reason the moment unlocked some feelings she was previously guarding.

"I really like you."

"I really like you, too."

"Even though I was raised Catholic?" she quipped.

"About that...."

She cut me off with a grin, "Don't worry. I'm non-practicing."

"So do you want my help this weekend?"

"Sure; the perfect spa for twelve girls isn't going to pick out itself."

"I was thinking...."

"Sure, you can go car shopping with me."

Shannon and I spent Saturday meandering through used car lots, taking test drives, and kicking tires. No salesman with a loud tie offered us a chocolate croissant, but maybe not all great romantic comedies take place in cafes and art museums. Sometimes, what you need to find is reliable transportation. It certainly wasn't the sexiest date, but it was just the two of us: No Allie. No Craig. No Glen. From now on, no other party crashers were going to twist us into any new metaphorical polygons. What was once five now stood at two—a crowded quintet of romantic partners had been narrowed to an intimate duet. The love pentagram was no more.

CHAPTER 23

ICED COFFEE

Standing and waiting in line, I tapped my hand on my pocket against my wallet and keys. The upbeat rhythm and punchy lyrics of "Nightingale" were running through my head as I admired the military organization of arrays of crullers and checked out the latest promotions on the overhead pink and orange posters. I was at Dunkin Donuts, participating in one of my favorites rites of spring: the first iced coffee of the year. Once it was warm enough to roll down the car windows, I passed up my usual stop for hot coffee and opted for the colder version. It was my personal turning of the page and moving from winter's chilly darkness. A giant plastic cup filled with iced hazelnut may not have waxed as poetic as the first flowering white orchid, but it was my prayer of thanks for the season of hope and optimism. Walking back to the car with thirty-two ounces of delicious energizing nectar, I belted out the notes of God Street Wine's biggest hit, which became the morning's anthem for brighter days ahead.

Resuming my commute to school, I rewound the cassette so I could hear the whole song one more time before work. Perhaps it was the spirit of spring and the time of rebirth or maybe it was sipping iced coffee, but it felt like my relationship with Kelly's mixtape had changed. Even though it was my security blanket throughout the winter, listening to it often felt like penance, the heavy chords relentlessly punishing me for my loss. As much as the memories hurt, I had no choice but to surround myself with sorrowful sounds and wallow in resulting self-pity. But today, the music felt brighter, less burdensome, and more bittersweet. The notes or lyrics hadn't changed *but perhaps I had?*

Leaving my jacket in the car, I strolled toward the brick building, the lips of my smile occasionally parting for caffeine intake. There was no doubt about it: teaching at Greenridge was more fun after spring break. Summer was on the horizon, standardized testing was complete, and the mood lightened as we appreciated what had been accomplished over the past year. While it was the sixth-graders who were moving on to middle school, there were achievements to be celebrated at each grade level. Fourth-graders completed their "Regions of New Jersey" projects, third-graders mastered their times tables, and the kindergarteners had figured out how to insert a straw in a Capri Sun pouch without ejecting Tropical Punch all over the lunch table.

I was celebrating my own personal triumph as well. Back in October, I had no idea how I would survive. But somehow every morning I got out of bed, got dressed, and showed up for work. That school year will always be marked by personal tragedy, but I'll never forget my twenty-four first-grade coworkers who got me through that difficult time. They had no idea at the time, and probably never will, that just being their six year old selves—asking innocent questions, squirming in their seats, showing off their shoes and lunchboxes—helped me cope with my reality outside school. For that, I will always be particularly grateful for that class. By the time I was drinking iced coffee and wearing polos instead of long-sleeve dress shirts, life was starting to feel a little brighter.

Besides personal growth, a mundane but welcome benefit of spring was the Central New Jersey weather and its impact on recess duty. Several times a year, the faculty was assigned in pairs for week-long stints of playground supervision. Being a newer teacher, I had more tolerance for refereeing foursquare games and ensuring jungle gym fall victims got to the nurse. That being said, May is a delightful time to be sitting on the picnic tables next to the blacktop twirling a whistle; January, less so. It was a sunny Friday afternoon when Marlene Mitchell and I were completing our third and last tour of recess duty of the year. Marlene was a twenty-year-plus teaching veteran, and less enthusiastic about meeting her contractual obligation than I was. While I diligently surveyed the playing field, Marlene graded some third-grade reading packets.

"Look, look, look! It's happening!" I stage-whispered to Marlene, who looked up from behind her reading glasses.

"What's happening?" she asked somewhat annoyed.

"It's going down at the big slide."

Marlene removed her glasses and looked toward the southern end of the playground. At the base of the swing ladder, a boy and girl engaged in what looked like a serious conversation. These weren't the main players in the romantic game we were watching unfold, merely representatives sent to negotiate terms and shuttle messages back to their clients. The players in this dance, Jenny Samuels and Michael Robicheau, were on opposite ends of the playground, each surrounded by a posse of supporters and onlookers. This was the first proxy meeting of several, and I figured it would take most of recess to solidify a deal that would result in Michael asking Jenny to the sixth-grade dance.

Even a seasoned veteran like Marlene was amused by the annual adolescent mating ritual. "I had both of them in third grade," she proudly announced, cracking a smile. "Good kids, good families," she stated factually before going back to her grading.

I continued to monitor the sixth-grade drama and compared it to my recent romantic adventures. Unlike Jenny and Michael, I had outgrown the need for intermediaries, and I really didn't have a posse of supporters to cheerlead my love life. Navigating solo through the love pentagram, I hadn't postured or played games with Allie and Shannon; even if I wanted to, I don't know that I had the capacity after Kelly's death. For the past six months, my emotions were worn raw, completely exposed. There was a certain honesty to being that naked; I wasn't hiding behind any layers or guises.

I walked onto the blacktop, passed Michael's go-between, and gave him a little head nod—acknowledging the selfless yet ridiculous work he was doing. I was thankful not to be in sixth grade anymore. A warm breeze brushed across my face; I felt even more appreciation for the season: the green grass, the perfumed scent of lilacs, the cheerful cries of playing children. It was a time when a young teacher, even one on playground duty, could turn his attention to matters of the heart.

For the last two weeks, Shannon and I had engaged in a more formal courtship and things were going pretty well. I completed the *Shannon Reality Tour* of South Jersey: parents were met, high school stories recounted, and ice cream cones were shared. With Shannon back home for the summer, I got very familiar with a certain stretch of the New Jersey Turnpike. Right off her exit, there was a factory that made flavor additives. Even with the windows rolled up, as soon as I turned on to Route 73, my car was flooded with a generic candy aroma. The actual scent might have been strawberry or raspberry, but to me it smelled like anticipation and excitement.

Lost in thoughts of long spring evenings and flirtatious kisses outside her parents' house, I was snapped back to reality by an erupting kickball argument. I looked over to make sure tempers weren't overflowing to a point of needing adult intervention. Confident the dispute would resolve itself, a specific image of Shannon came to mind: her sitting on a rock in a stream. The previous week, we went on a hike and were trying to find a scenic spot to stop for lunch. I suggested a flat rock that required some effort to venture out to; Shannon responded with a comical skepticism. After stepping over some swirling eddies and almost falling in the water twice, Shannon smiled at me with a hint of superiority. Her expression suggested "You're such an idiot," but there was something else behind her grin as well. Throughout our meal of Wawa Shorti sandwiches, she flashed me that look several times. Her hair was backlit by the sun, and her eyes were illuminated with mischievous possibility. It was a perfect moment, and I loved everything about it. And I loved her.

Whoa! I loved her? That thought hadn't crossed my mind until just now. Searching my mind, heart, and soul, there was harmony and alignment among all three. *Wow! I loved Shannon!* At this particular moment of clarity, I was surrounded by girls skipping rope and boys shouting about POGs. While this may not have been the ideal time to come to this realization, love doesn't operate on a schedule. At least not for me. Jenny Samuels and Michael Robicheau had to fit their flirtations in between a geography test and a visit from their DARE officer.

Three sharp whistle blows interrupted my epiphany. Marlene had been watching the clock closer than I and signaled the end of recess. Students began lining up by the appropriate grade and class. As I walked back to the double red doors, my heart was full as was the grin on my face. *When would I tell her? What would she say? Does she love me, too?* The whistle blew again to collect the stragglers. Playtime was over. Kids had to get back to class, and I had just learned something about myself I didn't know at the beginning of recess. I couldn't wait for Shannon to find out as well.

CHAPTER 24

SAND HARBOR

A red traffic light of a sun hung in the sky above the tree line off the Garden State Parkway. Its crimson color against the dark blue sky was mesmerizing, a perfect orb gently retreating toward the horizon. Perhaps it was a signal to stop, but I was doing about seventy-five miles an hour to keep up with the northbound traffic. While the sun wouldn't set for a few more hours, the density and darkness of the Pine Barrens swallowed some of the late afternoon light, giving the coastal forest a mystical stillness to it. Although a steady flow of Memorial Day traffic motored through their woods, the permanence and resolve of the trees seemed to quiet the noise with an enchanted air.

Growing up, Shannon must have driven through Pinelands to go "down the shore" countless times. On this trip, she sat in my passenger seat and ran her fingers through her long, curly hair. Her eyes were guarded by tortoise-shell sunglasses and they gave me a look of recognition when she heard the first pop of snare drum from "Ants Marching." Exhausted from a fun weekend, we still mustered the energy to sing the Dave Matthews song, which would become ubiquitous that summer. We serenaded the skinny trunks of conifers standing in sandy soil, "People in every direction / No words exchanged / No time to exchange." After fumbling through the flood of words in the bridge section, we gave up and chuckled at our lyrical failure.

Even behind her sunglasses, I could see her eyes come alive when she laughed. There was an unbridled joy to her, a register of happiness I personally couldn't achieve, but one I liked to be around. Even before Kelly died, my overthinking and constant overanalyzing sapped me of personal contentment and general cheerfulness. Shannon didn't seem to have those problems. Not that she was shallow or vapid, but she was much more in the moment than I was. Listening to her laugh, admiring her eyes, holding her delicate hand kept me grounded in the present.

But tapping into those moments of staying present were fleeting for me. Sooner or later, my brain would always come along and wreck it. Even if it was with a good thought, it was still a thought that took us out of the moment we were presently enjoying. Sure enough, the evaluative process reared its analytical head. At least it was complimentary.

"This might be the best Memorial Day weekend I've ever had."

"Oh really?" she said, lowering her sunglasses.

"Well," I considered, "my Little League team won the championship when I was eleven. That was a pretty good time. I hit a triple, and we got ice cream afterward."

"A triple *and* ice cream?" Shannon continued to play along, "That beautiful memory has been knocked out of the top spot? Are you sure?"

Though her tone was laced with sarcasm, I sincerely considered her question and reflected on our time together since last Friday. Since leaving my apartment for the beach three days ago, I felt Shannon and I had grown closer—a connection I hoped she felt too. There was fullness in my heart and a brighter outlook on life, which I attributed to the graduate student in the passenger seat. I certainly had fond memories of that double scoop of mint chocolate chip and celebrating with the Watson Auto Part Tigers, but this weekend felt like a different kind of win.

Prior to Memorial Day weekend, Shannon had extended an invitation to her Aunt Eileen's beach house in Sand Harbor. Along the coast of New Jersey, there's a beach town for every economic status. If you were looking for a high concentration of tattoo parlors, mullets, and funnel cakes, Sand Harbor was not your destination. Sure, you could find arcades and candy shops on 3rd Avenue, but the fudge there cost a lot more than it did in Seaside Heights. The streets were lined with gray colonial houses with freshly painted white trim and American flags hanging off the front porch.

Aunt Eileen was family by choice, Mrs. Walsh's childhood friend from Philadelphia who married well, very well. Her summer house was a block from the beach and looked like something you'd find on the cover of a real estate magazine: a massive house sitting on the corner with a perfectly manicured lawn and landscaping. Unlike other stately manors tucked onto postage-stamp sized lots, this yard was big enough to display its patriotism from a twenty-five foot flag-pole surrounded by brick and flowers. When Shannon referred to our weekend host as her "rich aunt," she was not joking.

I barely got our bags out of the trunk when Aunt Eileen greeted us in her driveway, Bud Light in hand. She immediately pulled me in close before I could put down my suitcase. As she held me close to her chest, she did that thing older women do when they're hugging you and sort of hummed in my ear. It was a little weird, but I took it as a good and welcoming sign. She finally released me, smoothed out her designer tracksuit and adjusted her visor.

"I see a few wisps of clouds out there," she announced looking east, "should be a nice weekend."

"Aunt Eileen loves meteorology and predicting the weather for us," Shannon explained. "She was heartbroken when the Weather Channel became available on cable and put her out of a job."

"TV isn't always right," Eileen protested, "You remember that one time I told you it was going to rain, and I wouldn't let you and your brother go water skiing?"

"How could I forget it? You won't let us," Shannon said and endured a playful punch from Eileen and smiled broadly at our host.

"You two get yourself settled and make yourself at home. It's almost time for communion practice."

While we unpacked in the sixth guest bedroom, Shannon explained to me that *communion practice* referred to Eileen's daily cocktail hour that took place at four o'clock every afternoon on her second story deck.

"What are you having, James?" Eileen asked as she scooped some ice into a glass. "My husband makes a mean Manhattan, but I can't remember the recipe, so I'm drinking plain whiskey."

"Sounds good to me." Eileen nodded at a tray on the counter, gesturing for me to bring it outside. Her deck was a long par 5 away from the ocean, and while the view wasn't completely unobstructed, you could practically taste the lobster and clams. Our glasses touched and Eileen recited something that might have been from Ecclesiastes or Led Zeppelin.

"When is Uncle Jimmy coming down?" Shannon asked.

"Who knows?" Eileen said, grabbing a Triscuit from the tray. "I can't keep track of that man's schedule. That used to be your job when you were down here."

"Along with everything else," Shannon retorted.

Eileen sipped her whiskey and roughly pointed to me without taking her eyes off the ocean. "Shannon would come down in the summer and watch the twins. Best live-in nanny/chef/maid we've ever had. When the kids went to bed, she was my card partner and we'd clean up against the boys."

"You know it," the ex-nanny chimed in. Eileen and Shannon continued to share stories; I mainly listened and didn't add much conversation. After a while, I was pretty buzzed from Eileen's generous pours and felt relaxed with Shannon's adoptive family. There was something incredibly comfortable about Eileen. Her real estate suggested a tremendous amount of wealth, but her lack of pretentiousness could be seen in the generic potato chips and onion dip sitting on the table. Her sense of easiness and approachability was a quality that she shared with Shannon.

Welcomed by a gracious host and half-drunk a lot of the time, our weekend flew by. Shannon and I explored the beach, while Eileen sat on her deck and read her Danielle Steel novels and worked on *The Philadelphia Inquirer* crossword puzzle. As we sat on the beach, Shannon taught me how to tell the difference between locals and "shoobies," those visiting the beach for the day. Shoobies carted way too much stuff onto the sand and had a general look of disorientation. After a morning swim, we would ride bikes or play mini-golf, always ensuring we returned to the house in time for communion practice. For as laid-back and informal as Eileen was, you did not mess with her happy hour.

In addition to house guests, there were usually at least one or two neighbors in attendance on Eileen's deck. One of them, Barbara, became my nightly card partner as I was baptized into their regular game of Euchre. Barbara was a very nice woman and apparently one of the best senior tennis players in the area, but we didn't stand a chance. Eileen and her goddaughter played for blood. After a night of stiff drinks and being beaten badly in cards, the trash talking continued as we got under the covers for bed.

"So…you're not a very good card player," Shannon playfully mocked me, "You're kind of making me look bad."

"All I know is you invited me down here for a nice weekend at the beach, and it turns out you're hustling me. Tomorrow you're probably going to scam poor Barbara out of her pension money."

"Don't worry; we've beaten much better players."

What Shannon said was meant to be mildly insulting, but something about her in that moment absolutely captivated me. Her beauty was amplified by the sound of the surf and glow of moonlight; I was spellbound by her words, her smile, and her slight South Jersey accent. Everything about her was endearing and all of a sudden, it was the right time to tell her. Whether it was her confidence, the Jameson in my bloodstream, or the magic of the beach, my emotions rose to the surface, forming words that needed to escape their non-verbal prison. The pressure to express my feelings had reached its breaking point. I took a chance.

"Hey," I said, getting the attention of her olive eyes, "I love you."

Her eyes looked slightly away, but I could tell they lit up as she smiled. As she inhaled slowly, one hand touched her heart and her other found mine. She exhaled meaningfully and then looked me right in the eye.

"Me too."

Of all the possible responses to saying "I love you" to someone, it certainly wasn't the worst I'd ever heard. One time in college, I got a "thank you" from Robyn Engles, which she followed up with "It's nice to hear someone loves you." As it turned out, her "thank you" was really more a "No, thank you"—like I had offered her an unwanted serving of vegetables. I'd experienced my share of heartbreak, and hearing "Me too" was certainly better than someone treating you like a scoop full of lima beans. *But...why didn't she say, "I love you, too."* While it was disappointing she didn't say the actual words back to me, soon we were kissing passionately enough to take my mind off it.

I had said the words two days ago, and I had no regrets about doing so. Now, heading back to my place with the weekend winding down, I was filled with a rare sense of contentment—a feeling that didn't come easily to me. I loved her, and she loved me. Eventually, I was sure I would get her to say the actual words. Even though she hadn't said it, her actions indicated it.

As she reached into her purse for a stick of gum, I caught a glimpse of her chipped manicure and her Claddagh ring on her right hand. At some point this weekend, she had turned her ring around, signifying the ring-wearer is in a relationship. I hadn't noticed when Shannon had done that, but previously she wore it with the heart pointing out. From past conversations, I knew the ring and its positioning meant a lot to her—the orientation of the ring's heart as well as her heart was not an accident.

Our hands grazed each other, and we shared a smile. For a stretch of the road, I was able to enjoy the moment without overthinking it. So often, my stream of consciousness was unnecessarily overreaching, but for now my thoughts were relatively simple: *This is nice. It feels good.*

Of course, even my simplest thoughts tend to give birth to more complex ones. Pretty soon, my brain craved to distill more meaning. *I'm aware of how this moment is fleeting, like the red sunlight sifting through the dark tree branches.* Just because I thought too much, didn't mean I couldn't be poetic.

It was hard for me to truly live in the present but to escape the clutches of the past felt like progress. People like Shannon are able to stay centered and grounded, not worrying too much about the past or the future. I always had unnecessary regret and anticipation running through my brain, feeding me like a crawling news ticker. But for right now, I was doing my best to keep the pace of that chyron to a minimum. After an amazing weekend, I was driving home on the Parkway with the woman I loved. Like the sun, fighting not to disappear below the horizon, I wanted this moment to linger. I was nostalgic for the present.

CHAPTER 25

CURSIVE WRITING

The cursive writing was perfect, the product of each arc and loop having been practiced over and over in Mrs. Cavanaugh's third-grade classroom. The meticulous formation, spacing, and slant of each word could have been examples from a penmanship textbook. Inside the front cover was a short inscription:

James-

The words within have a lot of meaning to me. I hope you find them meaningful, too.

Love,

Shannon

The book was *The Prophet* by Kahlil Gibran, and it was a birthday gift to me. We were celebrating at The Rusty Grille, a casual restaurant off Route 1. It was decorated with a dark brown and copper palette that was much hipper than the surrounding family-owned diners and corporate establishments. I thanked Shannon for the gift and started thumbing through the pages.

"Have you read it?" she asked.

"No, I haven't," I said, looking back at her letter-perfect script.

"I thought you'd like it because you were a philosophy major in college. Give that big brain of yours something to dig into."

As she spoke, I examined the little heart she drew before the word "love" which reminded me of her ring. Then, I fixated on the word "love," tracing the curves of the letters with my eyes and imagining Shannon writing the word herself. A scene from Sand Harbor and telling Shannon I loved her popped into my head, and insecurity started bubbling to the surface. I didn't want it to, but I couldn't help it. My big brain that would revel in the poems of *The Prophet* wasn't driving; my nine-year old self grabbed the wheel. The smallest, pettiest version of myself was about to make an appearance at my birthday dinner. Apprehension registered on my face; Shannon read the change in my expression.

"Is something wrong? Do you not like the book?"

"No, it's not that. It's...a...it's something else." I was still fighting, still resisting Little James, hoping I could keep him at bay.

"What is it?" *Why did she have to ask?* It was useless. Big Brain James couldn't take back control. I was going to say it, had to say it.

"Well, last weekend, when I told you I loved you, you didn't say it back."

"I thought I did."

"You said, 'me too,' but you didn't say, 'I love you.'" *God, I was putting her on trial.* Let the record show that the witness said, "Me too."

Shannon squirmed in her seat, "Is that important?"

"I think it is," I mused. She took my hand, leaned to me to specifically make eye contact with my lowered gaze.

"I do love you." It felt good to hear her say that—but not as good as if it would have been spontaneous. Felt more like a legal counter argument than a spontaneous expression of emotion. "I don't know why I didn't say it the other night. I'm here. I'm all in on this thing. I hope you don't have any doubts about that."

"I don't." And I didn't. "I just needed to hear you say it."

"I love you," she repeated for emphasis.

"I love you, too."

Right at that second, a gaggle of waiters delivered a sundae to our table, adorned with a sparkler and accompanied by a woefully unenthusiastic birthday song. As they uncomfortably serenaded us while ice cream ran down the side of a warmed brownie, Shannon flashed me a little smile. It wasn't her 1000-watt smile; it was a forced grin, its usual radiance diminished. The "Why didn't you say you loved me back" deposition had sucked the joy out of what should have been a happier occasion.

That's my superpower—I can talk anything to death. No one's present contentment is safe if James thinks some rigorous analysis and Socratic dialogue is going to achieve a new level of collective understanding. Picking at the remains of the ice cream, I could feel myself doing it, but I couldn't help myself. I had wrecked a Sand

Harbor memory from the past and killed the moment in the present; I might as well try to damage the future.

I sat up and gestured with my spoon like the staff of a tribal leader. "So how is this going to work when you're in Ohio?" The question caught her off guard with dessert in her mouth. She held up a finger and nodded to indicate she needed to finish chewing.

"It's a pretty short flight from Newark to Columbus. If we can't afford to fly, we'll make the drive now and then. My parents will definitely expect me to be home for Thanksgiving and Christmas."

The thought of Shannon 500 miles away and the prospect of a long-distance relationship were less than appealing. I had recently stored my heart in Boston for several months, and I wasn't thrilled about the prospect of shipping it off to Columbus. Ultimately, I don't think it was the distance that doomed Allie and me, but I understood all too well the conflicting pull of having my love life and real life rooted in separate worlds. She had too.

"I'm guessing you and Craig had the same kind of conversations about weekend flights and holidays," I said without thinking. "I don't want that to happen to us."

Shannon tilted her head to the side and paused for a beat. "We did, but even when we were both at Rutgers, he didn't make our relationship that much a priority. To be honest, there were a lot of times it felt like we were together when it was convenient for him." As she finished the thought, she nodded slowly up and down, as if this was a truth she was just now realizing and accepting.

"I'm sorry, I didn't mean to…"

"It's okay," she stopped me and took my hand. "This is different." Her light touch and genuine smile reassured me. I tried to strike a more positive tone.

"It is different," I reiterated, speaking for myself. I took a sip of water and tried to get out of my head. I couldn't do it. Thoughts of calendars and potential windows of time together popped in my brain.

"When do your classes start?"

"Right after the Fourth of July. I figured I would try to get out there a week or so early." Shannon detected my slight slump and added, "As much as I'd like to hang out in New Jersey, that master's in speech therapy isn't going to earn itself."

"What if I drove out there with you, helped you set up for a few days, and then flew back," I offered hastily.

"That's a lot of unnecessary travel. You don't have to do that."

"But I could. I could be the helpful boyfriend. You might need someone to hang up a picture or hook up your cable?"

"I think I can handle those things." My offer was light-hearted, but I still would have preferred her to say yes. Since she passed on my move-in pitch, I decided to swing for the fences.

"Or…," I mused while sort of pointing in the air, "and here's another idea: what if I spent the summer with you in Columbus?"

"Are you serious?"

I actually was. The thought hadn't occurred to me until that very moment, but once I spoke it into existence, it sounded like a good idea to me. I looked her directly in the eye to project confi-

dence. The busboy had cleared my tribal leader spoon, so any conviction or credibility had to come from within me.

"I am. Think about it. I have the summer off. I could get a job
in Columbus. I've got some curriculum work through the district,
but I can do that anywhere." With each sentence, I felt more determined that this is what should happen. "Plus, my high school friend,
Jeff, is getting married in Chicago. We could drive up for that."

Shannon sat still, silently considering the compelling arguments
that I had laid out before her. I was expecting more of an objec-
tion, but when she finally spoke, Shannon asked a relatively simple
question.

"You would want to do that?" she wondered, looking at me, her
eyes greener than usual.

I nodded affirmatively. "Absolutely I would." And she started
nodding back in agreement. A guilty grin started to creep across her
face, like she was getting away with something.

"So, what do we do?" she wondered.

"Let's make a list." I flipped over the receipt from dinner and
brainstormed what we would need to happen to make our summer
project a reality. Even though my potential Columbus sojourn
would only be eight weeks long, we itemized a number of logistics
including forwarding mail and figuring out if we could afford cable.

As our plans unfolded, her eyes sparkled with enthusiasm, as
if she were beginning to truly see this daring and ambitious idea
take shape in her mind. I wrote feverishly trying to document the
conversation. When it was time to go, I bookmarked the receipt
with the "meeting minutes" inside the copy of my new book—my

frenetic scribbling right next to Shannon's polished handwritten inscription. As the taper of the moon had begun its ascent, we strolled across the Rusty Grille parking lot to my car. In one arm, I held my new copy of *The Prophet* and Shannon's hand in the other. I glanced down at the book and the mystical images on the cover. I was looking forward to reading it. I was even more excited about what was written on that receipt.

CHAPTER 26

DOORWAYS

The current sixth graders stood on the risers in the combination gymnasium/cafeteria for the final time. They would be students at Greenridge for about another twenty hours. Sixth-grade promotion, our pseudo-graduation ceremony, was the evening before the last day of school. Our music teacher stood in front of them, directing them through the final chorus of "A Whole New World" from *Aladdin*. Mothers in the crowd teared up. Dads operated bulky video cameras. Younger siblings squirmed in metal folding chairs. A few of my students were in attendance with their families, and it felt foreign to be in that room without being responsible for their behavior. It didn't keep me from slyly shooting Matthew Angrelotti a look when he started giggling during his sister's solo.

After a robust round of applause, the sixth graders moved to their seats on stage and our principal stepped to a podium, trying to clap with one hand full of index cards. Shanice Jamison was a ball of energy fueled by positive ideology and anything chocolate. After making a joke about having to compose herself, she began her annual address to the students, a recycled version of the year before and the year before that:

"I haven't been principal for all of their time at Greenridge, but I can tell you this is an exceptional group of students. While we don't know where they will go from here, our hope is that within these walls, in these halls, and on this playground, they've learned the lessons they need to be successful moving forward."

After a polite ovation from the crowd, she turned to the students with a message more directed to them:

"You should celebrate this moment because it's a big deal. Many of you have been here since kindergarten. But even though your time at Greenridge is ending, something else is beginning. Next fall, you'll be starting seventh grade down the road. So right now, you find yourself in a doorway, elementary school on one side, middle school on the other. There's going to be a lot of times in life when you find yourself making similar transitions, moving from one stage of your life to another. Your first day of kindergarten was one of those doorways. Even though you may be scared or nervous, just remember the reason you're in the doorway is because you're ready to walk through it. You guys got this! And with that, allow me to present this year's sixth grade class of Greenridge Elementary."

As the room erupted into celebratory cheering, hopefully no parent noticed the young first-grade teacher welling up with tears. I surreptitiously swept the wetness from my eyes, pretending I was cleaning my glasses. Principal Jamison was a big fan of the doorway metaphor, and I had heard versions of it many times before. But this particular rendition—told at the end of a personally tragic school year—touched something within me, unexpectedly spilling open some of my emotional baggage. I thought about Kelly and how my life was cleaved at the point of her death, separating it into two mismatched pieces. Unlike the summer before middle school, her suicide created a completely unexpected transition. Was this my doorway: was Columbus on the other side of my sister dying?

By the time the last sixth-grade name was announced, the tears had stopped; thankfully, no one had witnessed my private moment of sorrow. The ceremony ended, giving way to the inevitable flurry of picture-taking and the coordination of celebratory family dinner plans. Near one end of the gym, a group of girls, huddled in an embrace, broke into an a capella version of "Water Runs Dry" by Boyz II Men, stopping periodically to weep in unison. Their sentimental spectacle not only blocked one of the exits, but was something the twelve-year-old boys in their short-sleeve dress shirts couldn't quite access or appreciate. I found myself feeling unusually judgmental of their snickering.

I typically enjoyed the sixth-grade promotion, seeing the oldest students in our school culminate their elementary school experience. But on this night, I was unsettled—shaken up like a snow globe jostled around before being set down to let the glitter flakes settle and land. My sister's presence at tonight's proceedings was unexpected; the program hadn't mentioned any dead relatives of the faculty. Shanice's speech was yet another one of the many emotional landmines Grief would litter throughout the rest of my life.

The following morning, the gym stood bare, with the decorations undone and the hundreds of folding chairs stored in racks under stage. I started my day with iced coffee, mixtape therapy, and a renewed sense of optimism. By the time Katelyn Everson skipped into my classroom, I was in a much better place to say goodbye to my students and families, who presented me with "thank you" gifts of cartoon character ties and coffee mugs stamped with obvious humor. The last day of school was filled with more ritual: signing yearbooks, cleaning out desks, teachers completing childish checklists as a prerequisite of getting their last paycheck.

After the faculty waved to send off the last school bus at 3:15 p.m., teachers started packing up their rooms and saying their goodbyes for the summer. Staples fell to the floor as the last of the bulletin boards were uncovered. Classroom flags were rolled up and covered in craft paper. Teachers carted boxes and folders out to their cars. As I was carefully securing my district-approved computer into my front seat, Sheri walked by, putting a stack of Barnes & Noble gift cards from her fourth graders into her purse.

"Are you pretending you're going to work over the summer?" she joked.

"I signed up for curriculum work for the new math standards."

"They have to find some sucker to do that."

"Not all of us are so high up the pay scale," I said carefully, placing the seat belt around the monitor. "What about you?"

"Let me tell you about the exciting summer teacher life of a single mother. When I'm not chauffeuring my monsters to day camps or the beach, I'll be refereeing life and death disputes along the lines of 'who's touching whom in the back seat' and 'why didn't I get the red popsicle?' And on the off chance I do get to read by the pool, instead of some trashy novel, it will probably be an educational text about teaching literacy across multiple subjects." She feigned a smile and shrugged her shoulders in a resigned sort of way. Listening to her describe her life—overly scheduled if not trapped—was worlds apart from mine. I had so much freedom and discretion over my life sometimes it bored me. Sheri dug out her car keys, waited a beat, and asked me, "So you're really going to Columbus for the summer?"

Hearing Sheri state my vacation plans out loud made them seem silly if not childish. I don't think she was trying to be critical or patronizing, but the most practical part inside me inferred something from her question and immediately started sowing seeds of doubt. I spoke up to defend romance and refute pragmatism. My response was probably laced with too much anxiety and aggression.

"I know it might not make sense to someone else, but why shouldn't I go? What's keeping me here for the summer? I'd be miserable with more time on my hands. All I'd be doing is waiting for a time when we could see each other." The vigor of my rebuttal to an argument Sheri wasn't actually making surprised her. Her eyes widened a bit as her head tilted back.

"I think it's great that you're spending the summer together," she said reassuringly. "You should have all the fun and adventures you can before you're saddled with all this." As she said "this," her eyes found the direction of Sharon Elman, who was criticizing the way her two teenage children were carrying some classroom supplies to her Plymouth Voyager, providing critical feedback with almost every step.

Sheri's warning about suburban trappings in my future didn't quite resonate with me. I always thought minivans got a bad rap, and I could definitely envision myself someday coaching Little League, carting infielders and catcher's gear to the ballpark. She seemed to be making a "you're only young once" case for Columbus, but that wasn't why I was going.

"Well, I can't wait. Did you know that there's a new professional soccer league starting up and that Columbus has a team?"

"In all my free time," she said comically gesturing, "when would I brush up on franchises of a new professional soccer league?" She threw her arms in the air, exasperated with me. "Do you think there's a lot of *Sports Center* on my TV?" We shared a laugh and talked until the parking lot emptied out. A check of her watch prompted a sigh, and she was off to her role of ex-wife and mother. Sheri gave me a hug as we wished each other well for the summer.

I closed my passenger car door on my borrowed computer and looked back at the school building. *Doorways…Kelly…Shannon.* In years to come, I would catalog time by individual school years— my ability to recall news events or pop songs anchored to specific memories of particular classes and students. That was the year the Republicans took back the House, and everyone discovered Hootie and Blowfish, but for me, that particular class will be etched in my heart forever as one of the last links to the memory of my sister.

Our principal had a version of the doorway speech, which she typically gave right before the kids started back at school; she reminded us that teaching, unlike many other professions, has a natural rhythm of starts and stops. Each academic year is bookended by September and June; each first day of school represents a chance to begin again. Professionally, I entered my fourth year of teaching with boatloads of enthusiasm, convinced my first three years had pushed me far enough along the learning curve to do great things. On a personal level, it hadn't been a year of great things, and for obvious reasons, I was more than ready to say goodbye—to put a period at the end of this chapter. Like our newly promoted sixth-graders, my future was also full of new and unknown challenges. *Had I learned the lessons I needed to be successful moving forward? After a summer in Columbus, where would the doorway to the following school year find me?*

LIVING ON 10TH STREET

It looked like a toy, like something you would find in the kitchen play corner of a kindergarten classroom, sitting next to a wooden refrigerator along with stray pieces of plastic fruit. Sure enough, it was real, and although it was tiny, it absolutely needed to be, considering we didn't have much counter space to spare. Most importantly, it brewed coffee—not a lot of coffee—but the four-cup mini-carafe was enough for Shannon and me on most days. For $34.86, it was purchased at ValueMart along with a can opener, some measuring cups, and a rack to dry dishes. We went dutch on our new home furnishings, and our shiny new coffee maker represented our first ever joint purchase.

We carried our first home appliance along with several bags of groceries into a studio apartment on 10th Street, which was cheap, clean, and a short bike ride to campus. It was on the second floor of a U-shaped apartment building that opened up to a courtyard of picnic tables and barbecue grills. Without a backyard or balcony, residents displayed potted plants and stashed kids' bikes outside their front doors. Our compact kitchen with a two-burner stove and no dishwasher was so cramped we had to take turns standing in it. Our living space had room for a bed, a couch we found at a yard sale, and a desk I fashioned out of a piece of plywood and two sawhorses. Milk crates held Shannon's textbooks on motor speech disorders while my clothes lived in a pile on a suitcase in the corner.

It was by no means the most prestigious neighborhood I've ever lived in, which made sense given our vocations in life. Shannon was a graduate student; I was a teacher in the summertime. I did my best to stretch my ten months of paychecks over twelve, but July and August always seemed to be underfunded. So, our summer lifestyle was guided by purposeful frugality. We grilled portobello mushrooms instead of steaks. Dime wing night and shooting pool at Jake's Tavern represented high dining and culture. Our big-ticket splurge for entertainment was attending Columbus Crew matches during their inaugural season. For sixteen dollars we could sit in "the Horseshoe" and watch Major League soccer. It wasn't the lap of luxury, but we were happy to make do with what we had.

It didn't matter if we were checking out a new band across town or shopping for a used laptop computer for the graduate student, I was a giddy little kid getting to spend every day with her. Sure there is a certain loss of mystique when you start living together, the uncovering of certain personal habits that were previously unknown, but there's also tremendous intimacy in being comfortable enough to reveal your less-than-polished self to someone else. After a few days of Shannon turning her back to me as she undressed for bed, I decided to ask her about it.

"You know, I've seen you naked."

Shannon finished pulling a well-worn Scarlet Knights t-shirt over her head and let out a little sigh. She sat down next to me on the bed. With her head staring into my chest she admitted, "I'm a little insecure about my scar." She was referring to the evidence of her appendectomy, and I felt stupid for not thinking of that and my lack of empathy.

"I'm sorry. I completely forgot."

"It's really ugly," she said scrunching up her face, "Doubt you'd find it very attractive."

I put my hand on her thigh and tried to reassure her. "Hey, I love you and you don't have to hide any part of yourself if you don't want to." We exchanged knowing nods, and Shannon pulled up her red t-shirt, revealing the recovering incision on her abdomen. It wasn't nearly as bad as she made it out to be. I leaned over, kissed her, and whispered in the quiet space between us.

"I think you're beautiful."

She kissed me back, touched my face, and then lightened the mood to something more playful.

"Consider yourself warned: I am not going to be seen in a bikini this summer."

"That's okay; neither am I."

As we worked out the necessary interpersonal skills of sharing a bed and an address, I was able to find more work outside our home. Right before I left New Jersey, I got a call from Huntington Academy, a private day school in the wealthy northwest Columbus suburbs. I had applied to a few summer jobs, not expecting much response, but a kind voice identifying herself from the personnel department wanted to conduct a phone interview. After the prerequisite background check and fingerprinting, I got a gig teaching pre-algebra to rich kids for six weeks.

On Day One, I got up early and showered in our claustrophobic bathroom that was covered in coral and white tile. I dumped all of the coffee maker's efforts into my travel mug and started a second batch for Shannon. She was still asleep, and I planted a kiss on her cheek before softly closing our front door. Descending the stairs on the side of our building, I twirled my keys around my index finger and hummed a nondescript melody. I was a regular guy, living in Ohio, off to my new job.

My humble, gray, four-door sedan stuck out like a sore thumb in the Huntington parking lot. Not only did most of the students arrive in mommy's BMW or Mercedes, but the staff parking lot was full of nicer cars as well. The faculty of Huntington seemed to consist of two main demographics: wives of stock brokers or professionals who had made their fortunes from lucrative careers and now wanted to "give back." I'm not sure working at a school that had two pools and a four-star chef counted as "giving back," but they welcomed me into their fold.

The campus itself was the very picture of a quintessential East Coast private school: serious-looking stone buildings, beautifully manicured gardens surrounding statues, interiors ensconced in wood paneling and adorned with banners in the signature Huntington blue. My classroom for the summer, third on the left after the framed portrait of the school's founder, was much nicer than room 22 back at Greenridge. Sitting in a $200 chair overlooking a fountain, I kind of felt like I was educationally cheating on public schools with my fancy private school mistress. The poshness and opulence of my days at Huntington stood in contrast to the humility of our studio apartment lifestyle.

We celebrated the end of my first work week with pricy coffee drinks at Moose & Mug Coffee Roasters. Shannon took a sip on her iced caramel latte and asked about my students who didn't live in studio apartments.

"So what are the kids like?"

"Good. Obviously they've been spoiled their whole life so they're pretty entitled, but they're sweet and for the most part they want to do well."

"So you like teaching older kids?"

"I really do. If nothing else they have a more mature sense of humor. Comedy in first grade is all about funny voices and pretending to fall down. I made an exponent joke today that killed," I proudly announced.

Shannon laughed. "So it's all about finding a better audience."

"No," I mused, "As someone who's only taught primary grades, it's pretty life-changing to have a class where everyone can read. In first grade, every lesson is a literacy lesson."

"It sounds like you're enjoying it."

"Yeah, maybe I'd want to teach middle school someday."

Friday afternoon iced coffee became one of our summer routines I really looked forward to. I'd arrive first, order our drinks, and wait for that gorgeous head of hair to walk through the doorway at Mug & Moose. Friday was Shannon's light class day so I had to entertain myself other afternoons. Some days I sat at a bar and watched baseball. I would try to make a single beer last multiple innings. Other days, I'd try to find one of the many disc golf courses in Central Ohio. I didn't have the same marijuana intake that I did in Alabama, and I think my Frisbee game suffered as a result. In the evenings, I would sit at the plywood desk doing curriculum work while Shannon sat on the couch reading up on Dysphagia and Traumatic Brain Injury.

When it was time to go to bed, we usually turned in at the same time-our place was so small it was kind of impractical to do anything else. On the nights Shannon stayed up later to study, I might have closed my eyes, but it was darn near impossible to fall asleep with my roommate awake in our 500 square feet habitat. Fortunately, Shannon was a diligent student and didn't need to burn the midnight oil too often.

While our personal circadian rhythms were fairly aligned, it turns out we were not as compatible in the bedroom as I previously had thought. Up until Columbus, whenever Shannon stayed over at my place, it was safe to assume we were going to have sex. Now that we were co-habituating, the lovemaking schedule wasn't nearly as predictable. Until that summer, the difference in our appetites didn't have a chance to reveal itself.

She never had to say "no" out loud; her closed-off body language was easy enough to read. When I tried to nuzzle the nape of her neck, her muscles tightened and the increased rigidness and tension clearly communicated "not tonight." I'd turn my advances into a goodnight kiss on the cheek, like that was my intention all along, before retreating like a defeated general back to my side of the bed.

As my eyes traced the slits of light that filtered through Venetian blinds into our dark room, I told myself that there were adjustments and compromises that needed to be made when you move in with someone. But at the same time my brain was rationalizing Shannon's behavior, my heart was hurt and rejected. *I'm so in love with you, and I just want to display that physically. How could you not want to sleep with me?*

What I didn't fully understand then was how much I relied on sex to feel close, to maintain a sense of intimacy and connection. Maybe it was the loss of a loved one that made physical contact my coping mechanism for holding on to someone, physically and literally. While Shannon was able to lift up her shirt and show me her recovering wound, my emotional scars lingered beneath the surface, invisible to both her and, at times, even to me. Although I may have been blind to the motivation driving my inner needs, she was also bringing an unhealed psyche to our bedroom, one that made physical affection increasingly difficult for her. At the time, I had no idea that our sexual incompatibility was a symptom of a deeper discord, one that would gradually crescendo into something impossible to ignore.

CHAPTER 28

BUCKETS OF SUNSCREEN

As July turned to August, an unseasonably rainy stretch hit Central Ohio. Shannon started driving to campus, leaving her mountain bike behind, and I started eating lunch at Huntington inside instead of my usual outdoor spot overlooking football practice. But besides the weather, our summer life had fallen into a fairly regular routine: school during the week, chicken wings on Tuesday, and the occasional Columbus Crew game. Sex was still not as frequent as I would have preferred, but I was getting used to that rhythm as well.

Once the rain subsided, the speech and pathology graduate students held a picnic at Walnut Ridge Park, which wasn't too far from campus. It was your typical burgers and dogs affair with one of the few males in the program manning the grill. Everyone else contributed salads or desserts; Shannon and I brought chocolate chip cookies made in our "easy bake oven." Including everyone's partners, it was a group of about thirty congregating under the blue sunshade by the tennis courts.

Shannon introduced me to her classmates and their boyfriends. Everyone was either still in college or working on varying advanced degrees; I was the only one with an actual job. I sat at the end of a table eating potato salad and realized I was having trouble connecting with this crowd. It had nothing to do with not being from Ohio or not wanting to be a speech pathologist. I was old. Back at Greenridge, surrounded by middle-aged women, I felt like I was about the same age as the student teachers, and I was definitely young enough to relate to their lot in life. But with these graduate students who were maybe one or two years older than Shannon, I felt ancient in this setting. Their isolated graduate program, disconnected from the real world, kept them incubated in an academic youth I was no longer acquainted with.

I tried to stay engaged in conversations about course schedules and clinical fellowships, but my mind and eyes kept drifting to the other parts of the park. On a nearby soccer field, kids younger than my first graders were playing soccer, or at least attempting to. Based on the cleanliness of their jerseys and the newness of their cleats, it was probably their first go-around with organized sports. As the youth soccer mob swarmed around the ball, I was struck by the gallery of parents taking in the game.

The women wore sundresses over white t-shirts or overall shorts; the men donned weekend polos or the jersey of their favorite Buckeye player. They sat in folding chairs, doled out orange slices, and coated their pale children in buckets of sunscreen. Whenever their child's foot grazed the ball they cheered vigorously before returning to their conversations about real estate and school supplies. But, within this sideline scene, it was the comfortable, almost complacent smirks of the slightly overweight husbands that struck me from across the pitch, their superior smiles taunting me without them ever knowing it. They had beautiful wives, four-bedroom houses, and gas grills that fired up sirloins, not mushrooms. It dawned on me that these were the same married couples who lived in the milk carton suburbs of Super Cool City back on my classroom floor. A few months ago, I hated these people; now I wanted to be them.

I glanced down at my khaki shorts and GAP t-shirt and wondered if I could have fit in with the parents of the Red Rockets. A mix of envy and longing started to balloon inside me.

I was once again a freshman in high school and the soccer parents were the taller, older, smarter seniors who sat on their territorial brick wall at lunch. They became my role models and I instantly aspired to have everything they did. Back in ninth grade, I knew time and enough credits would earn me a spot on the "senior ledge," but now I had no idea when I would get a seat in a folding chair next to a youth soccer game.

For the past four years, I had conversations with young moms and dads at parent/teacher conferences and never once thought about sitting on their side of the table. Even though they were about the same age as the sideline parents, in my mind they were so much older. Their world seemed so different from mine. Now, watching rec soccer in Ohio, I could feel myself preparing for this next stage of life: *marriage, kids, orange slices, sunscreen—I'm ready.*

I didn't want to be at the picnic tables with the grad school crowd eating hummus; I wanted to be at the soccer field, cheering on my dandelion-picking son or daughter.

I looked over and spotted Shannon munching on some baby carrots and talking to a third-generation Ohio State alum. She wasn't wearing a sundress, but she looked stunning nonetheless in a plain tank top and her hair in a bushy ponytail. Someday, we'd be on the other side of the park, adjusting our child's shin guards and asking friends for a recommendation for a piano teacher. *I'm not saying we'll get married anytime soon, but she's where my journey was supposed to lead.* And who knows, maybe I'll get a full-time job at Huntington and we'll move out to Dublin. Perhaps I could drive the kids to school with me in the morning or if we'd prefer to keep them in public schools; that would be fine too.

I left picnic area number three with a certain resolve to metaphorically make it over to the other side of the soccer field someday. Holding hands with Shannon, I knew I had found the right person to take that journey with.

That night Shannon had to call her mom and talk at length about some drama involving two of her other sisters, so I stepped outside in order to give her some privacy. Our apartment courtyard was dimly lit, but my nose easily detected the Lucky Strike cigarette of our downstairs neighbor. Since the rain had stopped, Gladys had returned to her usual spot, smoking at one of the concrete tables and using an old tuna can for ashtray.

Gladys was sixty-seven years old, and her face looked like most of that time had been unforgiving. She lived alone and her evening routine consisted of watching Wheel of Fortune and then drinking a series of Wild Turkey and RC Cola cocktails. When she ran out of soda, she would head outside and smoke to keep the cigarette smell out of her apartment. Gladys typically could be found after dark at the same table having a conversation, sometimes with a neighbor, often by herself.

Over the past month, we had developed a cordial apartment neighbor relationship, and I figured I could take a turn as her sympathetic ear. I followed the scent of tobacco downstairs and waited for her to look up at me before gesturing toward her table. She clumsily pointed downward, inviting me into her world. There was no small talk with Gladys; you were abruptly thrust into her ramblings without any context or explanation.

"He was the best," she lamented, "just the best...." The loss in her life was evident, but now it was far enough removed that she only cried without tears. I didn't know the particulars; Gladys wasn't the type to share, and I wasn't about to ask. I offered her an understanding nod without understanding anything and she continued, "I didn't know...how I was supposed to know...I would have done it...he never asked. James, why didn't he ask?"

"I don't know, Gladys."

"Exactly right!" she piped up and pointed her cigarette directly at me. "No one could know, and now it's too late."

"...too late," I repeated. I had learned over the past few weeks that it was pointless to try to advance the conversation or ask any questions. If you sat down at Gladys' table, your role was to sit very still and to parrot her words without judgment or interpretation.

She drew on what was left of her Lucky Strike and softly closed her eyes before placing both hands on the table. Sometimes, she would enter into what appeared to be meditative states; I wasn't sure if she was summoning some great wisdom or falling asleep.

"Hold on," she offered after opening her eyes. "You've got to hold on."

I muttered her last words before standing up and leaving the table. Exchanging good night pleasantries wasn't necessary; she was already onto her next portion of her monologue, another sad soliloquy spoken into the darkness. Typically, I thought nothing of her drunk musings, but tonight something struck a chord within me. She and I were obviously bonded through loss; Gladys had chosen to make grief her life's work. As I walked up the stairs, I was a little shaken up, and I considered the events of the past twelve hours. Between the soccer parents and my downstairs neighbor, this Saturday presented me with two possible versions of the future. I needed to choose the one that included orange slices.

Shannon had just hung up the phone when I got back upstairs. "How's your mom?"

"She's okay. She's trying to mediate an argument between Cara and Elizabeth. I told her to stay out of it, but she can't help herself."

"I was out talking to Gladys."

"I heard you or I should say I heard her." We shook our heads in unison and shared our usual laugh about Gladys. The images of my Saturday played again through my head: baby carrots, clean soccer jerseys, the tuna can used for ashtray. I launched into a conversation that it probably wasn't time for.

"Do you think you'd like to live here in Columbus?'

"I don't know. Maybe. I guess it's all right. Why do you ask?" Shannon was already lost, not privy to the transcript of my thoughts over the course of the day.

"I was thinking when we were at the park, watching the soccer game. Seemed like a nice place to raise a family."

"You want to raise a family in Columbus?" Shannon was puzzled if not bordering on offended.

"Maybe. All I know is that when my friend Chris got married right after college I thought he was crazy and too young. Now his life doesn't seem so crazy." *I didn't have a womb, and yet my biological clock was apparently ticking.* "Elizabeth is engaged. You must think about marriage and kids?"

"Sure. Someday in the future." Her eyes were wide with fear and confusion.

"Well, let me ask you this. What are we doing this summer? Why are we living together?"

"You suggested it, and it sounded fun," throwing her hands up in the air like it was the obvious answer. I wished that she saw our living situation as more on purpose, as a precursor for something bigger.

"Don't you perhaps see this as like a step to something else?" I led the witness as hard as I could.

"Maybe," she considered, finally up to speed with the emotional ambush her boyfriend had sprung on her. Shannon looked at me directly in the eyes in hopes of reassuring me. "I am having a great summer. I'm so glad you came out. I literally just started this program. It's hard for me to think too far into the future."

What she said was completely intellectually fair; it hurt nonetheless. "Well, just so you know, I'm thinking about those things, and those thoughts include you." She reached out and placed her hand on my arm.

"It has to be okay if I'm not there yet."

I bit my bottom lip and nodded in a resolved way, accepting that this is where we were. After a couple more nods, I finally answered.

"It is."

But, in reality, it was not.

CHAPTER 29

STEAMBOAT

Chicago was designed to be the highlight of the summer. A high-school friend, Jeff, was getting married in late August and I was going to be in the wedding. Much of our scrimp-and-save Columbus lifestyle was designed to have enough funds for the long weekend filled with multiple events for out-of-town guests. In addition to the chance for me to see childhood friends, we viewed this trip like our own mini summer vacation. Shannon and I followed the directions to the arranged accommodations from the back of the wedding invitation, and we were not disappointed.

The lobby of The Windsor Hotel was impressive enough, a cavernous space three-stories high supported by elegant reflective columns. Floor-to-ceiling windows fed the room with natural light and the energy of the surrounding outside streets. The clerk behind the reception desk had just handed us our room keys, when I heard the familiar voice of our high school's shortstop echo from behind me.

"Steamboat!" It was a nickname that very few people used. One of them was Chris Mallory, who was now descending down a metal and glass staircase with his wife, Kim. They got married right after college and moved out to California, so Chris could pursue his dream to be a movie producer. He was affable, social, and had more determination than anyone else I've ever known. Without the benefit of e-mail and group text threads, he was the one who made sure we all stayed in touch with each other, so it was hardly surprising he was the first familiar face I'd run into.

After hugs and introductions, Chris immediately started his usual role of connecting the group further together.

"So Shannon, Steamboat tells me you went to Rutgers and now you're at Ohio State?"

"Yes, *Steamboat* has that correct," emphasizing the name was new to her. "I recently started a program in speech pathology."

"My mother's family is from outside Columbus, and I have a few cousins still around there—huge Buckeye fans."

"Rutgers isn't really known for its football program, so it will be a new experience for me to be at a tailgate where we might actually want to go inside the stadium and watch the game."

We all chuckled and Chris continued to play talk show host, asking questions and sharing anecdotes. It had been too long since I had been around him; it felt comfortable to be in his orbit.

"This place is unbelievable," I said, admiring the size and scope of an abstract painting on square canvas that had to be at least twenty feet on each side. "This is where the wedding is going to be?"

"Yes," Chris nodded. "There's a rooftop deck where the ceremony will take place. Tremendous views of the city."

"Of course he had to go upstairs and check it out," Kim added. "Like he needs to approve the space or something." Her needling led to her husband giving her a loving slap upside the head.

"I'm sure he's taking his role as groomsman very seriously," I joked.

"As always," Kim agreed.

"Have you guys seen Jeff yet?" I inquired.

"Very briefly," Chris answered. "He and Amber were in the midst of running some wedding errands."

After a little more small talk, Chris' wandering eyes scanned for the next social opportunity. Not seeing one, he took to creating one himself. Extending his arms outward, he suggested, "What do you say we take this party into the hotel bar?"

Before we could all agree, Shannon said, "Why don't you guys go ahead. I was going to duck out and shop for a couple things I forgot."

"Is it alright if I join you?" Kim asked with a slight head tilt. "I packed one pair of shoes for the rehearsal dinner, but I don't love them. I was hoping to perhaps find a pair I might like better."

"Of course."

With that, Shannon and Kim ventured out onto Michigan Avenue for hair accessories and strappy sandals. The hotel lounge, The Meridian, was refined but relaxed; while a grand piano rested in the corner, the Cubs game was on most of the televisions behind the bar. Within five minutes of sitting down, Chris had learned names of both bartenders and let them know we were in town for a wedding. We ordered beers, toasted to friends, and reminisced about our glory days of playing baseball. Sprinkled in among the life updates was the announcement that in the fall they were hoping to buy their first house. Chris was on his way to becoming one of those suburban soccer dads—heck he'll probably be coaching the team. After about half a beer and a deep breath, he steered the conversation beyond yearbook references and professional resumes.

"Steamboat," he said with a specific note of sincerity. "I am so sorry I didn't make it to Kelly's funeral. We were on a stretch of this film and if I had taken any time off, I would have been fired." A half beat passed and he added, "And looking back, I wish that I had."

Seeing the earnestness in Chris' eyes, I was taken aback by his remorseful admission. "I've told you already; it's nothing you have to apologize for. You and I spoke shortly after, and I felt incredibly loved and supported by those who could make it."

"Maybe not, but I should have been there...I needed to be there. I mean, this was your sister! She was at every single one of our games." Then he added, "Granted she never watched the game, but I can't wrap my head around that the little girl sketching in the bleachers is gone." As he spoke, he reinforced his disbelief by sorrowfully shaking his head.

Whether he knew it or not, Chris' perspective stirred up a buffet of unexpected and conflicting emotions in me. On one hand, I was certainly affected that he referred to Kelly in the past tense, but I guess that was factually correct. Once again, I was shaken by the permanence of loss, but it wasn't a seismic jolt, just a minor aftershock. *Do we ever get used to not referring to loved ones in the present tense?* At the same time, I was weirdly comforted by Chris' regret over not storming off some sound stage in LA to make it back for the funeral. I had no idea how much Kelly's passing had touched my friend. Like so many other people—more than I would ever know—he knew her and loved her.

Chris could see I was staring at my beer and lost in this pool of thoughts.

"Oh, my god, Steamboat, is it okay that I'm talking about this stuff?"

I felt guilty about temporarily withdrawing from the conversation and not being accessible to my friend. "Of course it is. I appreciate it, man. I don't have enough chances to talk about her, you know? No one in my everyday life knew her." Immediately, I was flooded with memories, happy to be sitting next to someone who could indulge in them with me. "Do you remember the time she was practicing back walkovers in the grass and almost got hit with a foul ball?"

"Yes!" Chris laughed and pointed. "Coach Johnson was so mad at her for being at a baseball game and not paying attention. I think he yelled at her harder than he yelled at any of us that day."

"I think you're right." I spun a couple more classic Kelly anecdotes, and Chris was a good audience for my mediocre storytelling. We relived more childhood stories in between critiquing the unique windup motion of the Cubs starting pitcher.

"I spoke to Joel and Evan after the funeral. They said they saw the usual suspects. Anyone unexpected from high school make it back?"

Chris had just teed me up to tell him all about Allie. He was in Mrs. Barron's class. He was familiar with the artistic girl sitting in the back row of AP English and would have loved to hear about my adventures in Boston. For a second, I was about to blurt out the whole story, but something held me back. I hadn't told any of my friends about my whirlwind romance with my middle school crush. There was an aspect about that relationship that was secret, kind of existed in a vacuum, and that's what made it thrilling. Even though it was the fairly recent past, I intuitively knew those memories were meant to stay sealed. I was about to spend the weekend with a dozen or so people who would have loved to hear the sensational tales of Allie Lockwood, especially after a few drinks. But I kept those stories to myself. It wasn't important. Not to mention, the last thing Shannon needed to hear was all my idiot friends from high school saying, "Dude! You hooked up with *Allie Lockwood?*" Fortunately, Chris was ready to discuss my current relationship.

"Things are going well with Shannon? She seems great."

"Yeah, things are going great.... I mean, we've had an amazing summer. I think it's pretty serious." This might have been an exaggeration of relationship status, but I could be serious enough about us for the both of us.

"That's awesome. Steamboat, I'm really happy for you. You deserve it."

We re-toasted our glasses as I pondered what I did or didn't deserve. Chris was being nice and when he said "You deserve it," that was a commonplace thing to say to someone who was in a relatively new relationship. *But...was he consciously saying it in connection to the earlier part of our conversation about Kelly?* I reconsidered telling him about Allie, the love pentagram, and how this past winter all I

218

could think about was how much the universe owed me. That conversation would wait for another day, another setting with a round of scotches instead of beers. For the moment at the bar, on the cusp of Jeff's wedding, I assumed positive intent and allowed myself to enjoy Chris' happiness about my own life.

By the time we were multiple beers in and attempting to recount the entire cast of our fourth grade production of *Sleeping Beauty*, Shannon and Kim returned from their shopping excursion. They proudly showed off their newly purchased wares and retold a funny story about a street performer who failed at an attempted card trick, which they were both still pretty amused about. We transitioned to martinis, moved over to a booth, and established that the phrase "It should have been the eight of spades" would become a running joke for the weekend.

Familiar faces of Jeff's extended family started filling the cocktail lounge at The Meridian. Pretty soon, we were joined by the entire groom's side of the bridal party. Among them were Joel, who drove all night after a law school exam to make it to the funeral, and Evan, who famously told me I was able to "live with ambiguity." I had reached a loud, affectionate version of being drunk, and to me, every Fenwick-Merrill alum who walked through the door was a small miracle, worthy of bear hugs and ensuring Shannon knew their significant contributions to our graduating class. Fortunately, she was amused to hear my descriptions of Max Richmond's perfect SAT scores and how I threw a football at a plumbing truck that happened to be driven by Molly Torrillo's father.

At the same time, I couldn't refrain from letting Shannon know how I felt about her. I put an arm round and endearingly admired the little scar on her bottom lip. *God she was beautiful.* I kissed her on the little scar and finished telling her about Nick Alberetti playing "Tom Sawyer" on the drums in the eighth-grade talent show. She listened to every one of my dumb stories with wide eyes and an entertained smile.

"I love you."

"I love you, too."

Surrounded by good friends and with my arm around the woman I loved, I felt energized and invincible. The last time some of these people saw me was back in a community church on E. Genesee Street—the absolute lowest point of my life. Now, ten months later and 600 miles further west, things were different. Perhaps the universe had actually tipped the scales in my favor, providing a positive counterbalance to the heavy burden of personal loss I'd been carrying. Somewhere within that cocoon of old friends abuzz with the pre-wedding excitement, a strange feeling rose within me which I hadn't encountered in quite some time. Upon finishing a loud drunken chorus of our alma mater, I was finally able to put my finger on it.

It was a sense of peace.

CHAPTER 30

THE THRESHOLD

That sense of peace was very short-lived.

The next morning brought with it a relentless throbbing in my forehead, hammering against my skull. In addition to my headache, there was an uneasy swirl of memories from the night before bandying about my brain. After the last call at The Meridian, the out-of-towners retired to their hotel rooms. Shannon and I traversed the now vacant lobby with Chris and Kim at two in the morning, our laughter filling the empty space. As soon as the Mallorys got off the elevator on the eleventh floor, our time together in Chicago took an immediate turn for the worse.

Her predictable rejection of my physical advances prompted a switch to a more intellectual appeal. I made the observation that I had never had sex in Illinois, and this seemed as good a time as any to check the state off the map. As Shannon ambivalently leaned against the elevator railing, she was no more interested in a geography lesson than she was in any physical intimacy. Still, she steadied me on our walk down the hallway and ensured I made a soft landing on our bed among the oversized decorative pillows. A bottle of water arrived on the nightstand, and she started untying one of my shoes. Shannon was taking excellent care of her drunk boyfriend, but it wasn't enough for me. I wanted more.

"Do you think we'll wind up together?" I mused at the ceiling, slurring most of my words. "I think we'll wind up together. Someday, we'll get married like Jeff and Amber, probably not in Chicago though."

"Maybe…," she murmured, tossing one of my shoes aside.

Even though my mind wasn't its sharpest, her attempts to placate me were obvious enough. I propped myself on my elbows and looked around the room, slightly forgetting where I was. "Hey. Why don't you ever want to have a conversation about what's next for us?"

"You're drunk."

"I am," I conceded, "but it's still true."

"I don't know if this is the best time to talk about this."

"It's never a good time. You don't like talking about stuff like this."

"No," she said empathetically, "I don't like talking about it as much as you do." Blood started coloring the complexion of her face. I had pushed her too far, but I wasn't cognizant enough to realize it.

"Well, I thi—"

"Stop it!" she commanded. Her volume and tone shocked me into attention. My eyes followed her as she stomped toward the window, clenching and unclenching her fists, like she was trying to wring out her anger like water from a towel. She shook her head back and

forth before cradling it in both hands. "Listen. I can't have this conversation tonight. It's late and I'm going to bed. You should, too."

Other times, such a scolding would have fueled me with enough
anger to argue all night, but the martinis in my system dulled the
blades of any axes I wanted to grind. I searched for something smart
to say, tilting my head back and forth as if a good idea might happen
to spill out. Shannon went into the bathroom and brushed her teeth
as angrily as one can. Eventually, unable to find any new evidence to
present, I slid backward onto my pillow and chose to rest my case.

I woke up lying on top of the sheets in the clothes I was wearing the night before. Sitting up on the edge of the bed, I scooped up
the bottle of water as well as the three aspirin that were put out for
me. The Chicago skyline stared back at me unforgivingly as I drank
and thought about our argument from the night before, hearing it
for the first time in a sober state. As I assessed the damage, I didn't
realize Shannon was awake and doing the same.

"How's your head?"

I ran my fingers through my hair before looking back at her. "It'll
be okay. You?" She was leaning back in bed with her hands crossed
on top of the sheets.

"I'm sorry I yelled at you last night, but you have got to give
me a break."

"Give you a break?"

"Put yourself in my shoes. I'm at this event with all your friends.
It's a four-day wedding-o-rama. You know everyone here from high
school, and everyone loves you. I'm an outsider. I don't think now
is the time to give me the full court press on our relationship." She

obviously put some thought into her opening conversation this morning. I nodded and she continued, "I'm twenty-two years old. I have no idea what's next for me. Your friends are great, but you're all older. I should be allowed to be where I am in life." As she spoke, her big eyes were filled with honesty and trepidation.

I exhaled, considering her latest explanation of her not being ready for bigger things. *Why couldn't she see the future I saw? Why weren't we enough for her? Why wasn't she ready?* I considered our age difference: a five-year age gap is a finite duration of time, but particular stages of life carry different contexts. If I was nineteen, it would be criminal, and if I was fifty or even forty, no one would bat an eye. But, right now, Shannon and I sat on either side of our twenties, and the divide between us was apparent. I remembered being her age sitting in the pews at St. Mary's at Chris and Kim's wedding, thinking they were crazy for getting married right out of college. Back then, I knew in my core I certainly wasn't ready for the commitment they were making. Now, I expected Shannon to see the same future I did on the horizon, despite having less life experience.

"Well, this is where I am." I stated with conviction. "While I don't see my friends that often, these people know me better than anyone else in the whole world, and I truly feel like myself when I'm with them. Being around them gives me the confidence to know exactly what I want out of life, and what I want is to be with you."

It was the kind of speech that made women swoon in the movies, yet Shannon was unmoved. She lowered her head and looked down at her folded hands. "I know," she said with a resigned face. "Maybe you don't have to tell me about it all the time?"

"Why?" I questioned, and I heard the agitated edge to my voice. Although still weakened by my hangover, the anger slowly started to wake inside of me. *Shannon's problem was that she was with someone who told her too much that they wanted to be with her?* "Why wouldn't I tell you? Who am I supposed to tell?"

"I don't know. I've never been with anyone who wanted to talk so much about the future of a relationship."

"Maybe you've never been in an adult relationship." *That felt satisfying.* Now I was awake and *mad*. So was Shannon. She ripped off the covers, stood up and jabbed a finger in my direction.

"Goddammit! What the hell are you doing? I ask you for a break from this crap and you throw *I've never had an adult relationship* in my face? Jesus Christ, James, not everyone can be such a fucking enlightened twenty-seven year old. It must be difficult to be so old and so wise, but luckily you're surrounded by people who know you so goddamn well. Maybe you can stay here and hang out with the grownups, and I can go back to Columbus until I've matured enough!"

It was the kind of speech that didn't make anyone swoon, but it was effective nonetheless. I felt guilty, attacked, and a little turned on looking at her bare legs. Walking over to her side of the bed, I held up my hands in a conciliatory fashion and tried to soften my gaze toward her.

"Hey... I'm sorry. I shouldn't have said that. Don't go. I want you to be here."

Deep breaths escaped her fuming body. She was calming, but certainly not calm.

"I can't talk about this anymore."

"I know…I know. Can we hit pause on this and just try to get through brunch? It really means a lot to me that you're here. Please don't go."

"Fine," she agreed.

We got ready in relative silence, speaking sporadically to negotiate shower time and locate the camera we brought. Upon stepping out into the hallway, we found ourselves face-to-face with Jeff's sister and her family, two kids in tow. Shannon and I put on brave smiles, exchanged morning pleasantries, and successfully compartmentalized our earlier conflict. While the baby in the stroller might have sensed something was emotionally amiss, everyone else was too wrapped up in the weekend's excitement to notice any cracks in our relationship facade.

We carried on our act as the "happy couple" during the high-school brunch in the hotel restaurant, reliving last night's nonsense and embellishing childhood stories. The funny thing was: it wasn't really an act; we genuinely enjoyed each other's company. Shannon laughed at all the right places during Joel's midnight bowling anecdote; she threw in a few playful digs about my awkward attempts at flirting while she was student teaching. Sinking a fork into my Belgian waffle, my heart was filled with affection for her and she flashed me a little smile framed by her clear complexion. *Why were we so great at breakfast and not so good in the bedroom?*

The door to Room 1428 at the Windsor Hotel became a threshold separating two very different worlds that weekend. Beyond it, there were mimosas, tapas, and cheerful wedding guests. Inside, there was pain, conflict, and a never-ending litany of awkward discussions. Our hotel doorway was not the hopeful gateway of Principal Jameson's sixth-grade promotion speech; it was the divide between marital enthusiasm and unresolved pain.

Naively, I kept thinking we could get behind closed doors and talk ourselves into a better place, but the mood and atmosphere of that hotel room never improved. When Shannon and I were among a group of people, we were delightful and charming. But when we found ourselves alone, the worst versions of ourselves took over and picked up the ongoing argument wherever it left off.

That's how our time at Jeff's wedding went: two conflicting faces of our relationship playing out on opposite sides of that doorway. During my first ever trip to Chicago, I was able to take in all the major tourist attractions and landmarks of the Windy City, but I never did have sex in Illinois.

CHAPTER 31

THE BIG DAY

For the next three days, Shannon and I endured an exhaustingly recurring loop of public celebrations and private arguments. We'd escape to the next social gathering on the wedding agenda, only to return to the weight and tension of our unresolved discussions. The relationship claustrophobia of our hotel room got so stifling that we showed up thirty minutes early for every event that weekend, seeking new faces, emotional relief, or a stiff cocktail. No matter how well we got along while celebrating the future Mr. & Mrs. Sanderson, as soon as that key card hit the door, I would inevitably find a way to wreck the mood.

Friday afternoon, the wedding party hopped on the Red Line to Wrigley Field for a day game. Already buzzed from brunch after a couple overpriced beers, we were fully immersed in the festive stadium atmosphere. Chris orchestrated a game of Moundball, which involved gambling on whether a baseball that was returned to the pitcher's mound at the end of each half inning stayed on the dirt or trickled back in the infield grass. Shannon wasn't paying attention when she won $18 in the fifth inning, and her surprised smile and resulting laughter made my heart leap softly. As she sheepishly snatched the dollar bills from the empty beer cup, I was captivated, wishing I could freeze that moment and take it back to the hotel with us. When she glanced at me, showing off her newfound winnings, I thought I saw the same unspoken longing reflected in her eyes.

Any mutual affinity we had for each other waned by the time we got off the "L" and completely evaporated after another failed attempt at intimacy. She was retrieving something from her suitcase, and I caught her in an ambivalent hug and tried to escalate the embrace into something more. As I peppered her cheek with increasingly slower kisses, she immediately withdrew.

"Not now," she objected, retreating a step away from me.

"Then when?" I asked with a decidedly sharp edge to my voice. "It kind of seems like it's never the right time." I was angry from yet another rejection.

She countered with, "It kind of seems like you think it's always the right time."

Hard to argue with that. The truth was, our appetites were significantly different, and in Chicago, she wasn't offering even the smallest rations—I was being starved out. "This was supposed to be our vacation for the summer. I want us to feel close." My attempt at vulnerability did not land. An exasperated expression washed over her face and she turned away from me, throwing up her hands in frustration.

"I'm not in that place right now." She said looking over her shoulder. That was abundantly obvious; the question was, why?

"You know, it's not just sex. You won't even let me near you—show you affection of any kind. You and I are genuinely having fun together when we go out, but you can't stand to be alone with me. It's like you'd be more comfortable if we were friends." *Ooh...I think I might be onto something.* It was the first time I ever put that thought into words; the clarity didn't make them any less painful.

She wheeled around and shook her head at me, her long curly hair waving about her. An intense redness filled her face and the disgusted expression suggested I didn't understand how she was feeling, but I was supposed to.

"I can't right now. This whole weekend is...different." I was pretty sure it was the lack of love and affection, but I decided to keep that observation to myself.

"Is it me? Are you saying that I'm different?"

She paused. "No...it's not you." Then she gestured with arms, supposedly circling the wedding weekend. "This is a lot to be around. This weekend is filled with happy couples, and I'm feeling all this pressure that I'm supposed to be one of them."

"Are you saying that we're not happy?" I challenged her with a slightly accusatory tone.

"No, it's not that. It's that they're all so settled in their lives. They're married...or engaged...or doctors. I'm a graduate student eating ramen and driving a beat-up used car. I know you're not doing this on purpose and this is my stuff, but every time you come near me, I sense that you want me to be just like them. But I'm not." Reluctant tears started streaming down her face.

It turns out my high-school friends were her version of soccer parents. The difference between us was that while I was ready to cross the field to join them, she wanted to observe the game from the opposite sideline. The question was *how hard was I pushing her across the field?* Bringing her to Jeff's wedding wasn't a purposeful sales pitch for married life, but clearly whatever was being offered, she wasn't buying. Legend had it that weddings acted as aphrodisiacs for young women; this one seemed to be having the opposite effect on Shannon.

It was the perfect time to choose the high road. I could have asked her to sit down on the bed, rubbed her back, and offered something reassuring about being her own judge of success and progress in life. But no, I instead chose to be profoundly insulted by her "Every time you come near me…" line. My wounds were too deep not to lash out in retaliation. I couldn't help myself and slammed this particular conversation shut with a sarcastic apology.

"I'm sorry that my presence is such a burden to you."

Our roller coaster through Chicago continued through a group walk down Navy Pier, the rehearsal dinner, and a series of quarrels in between. By the time Saturday rolled around, we had run out of arguments to have. Prior to the ceremony, I had to meet up with the rest of the groomsmen to take pictures. Shannon was applying eye shadow when I appeared in the door frame of the bathroom in my rented tuxedo, with my hands joined contritely in front of me.

"Listen, I can't fight with you anymore, but there's something I have to say. You don't have to respond if you don't want to." She lowered her brush and her eyes widened with anticipation. Trying to recall the exact phrasing I had rehearsed in my head, I bit my lip and closed my eyes for two beats. "Shannon, I love you and I'm in love with you. Whenever I look at you, I feel something so powerful I can barely contain it inside me. I know what I want. I've tried to tell you, show you, convince you of this, thinking I could utter some magic words or stumble into some grand gesture that would make you love me enough. I was blind, and I assumed you wanted to take the next steps." I exhaled trying to steady my shaking legs before calmly uttering the sentence that had been ruminating in my head all afternoon, "If you don't see a future with us together, I'm not sure why we're together now."

She was emotionally spent; too much had been said and too many tears had been cried. Without a sound, she nodded her head in resigned acceptance.

Fortunately, I didn't encounter any members of the wedding party or any families pushing strollers on my way to the elevator. If I had, there was no way I could have concealed what had just transpired. I spent the twenty-five floor ascent determined to throw off the yolk of discontent, focus on my friends, and specifically to be there for Jeff. Whatever I was going through I would keep to myself; two days of stashing any uncomfortable feelings in a hotel room had prepared me for this. It was Jeff's big day, and I wasn't about to hijack it with my relationship drama.

The rooftop deck had been transformed from a utilitarian con-crete structure into something straight out of the pages of *Modern Bride*. Satin and lace draped over precise rows of white folding chairs, all set against the backdrop of Chicago's radiant, smiling afternoon sun. When the DJ started his pre-wedding playlist of saccharine-sweet love songs, I took my place beside the flowered arch, sandwiched between two high-school classmates. Shannon was sitting on the end of the third row next to Kim. Her hair was pulled back, exposing a pair of gold and pearl earrings against her delicate neck. The occasion called for a more dramatic shade of lip-stick, which contrasted her fair complexion more than usual. She was easily the most beautiful woman in the room.

As the ceremony drew on, she became my singular focus. It started with a sly glance, but during the second reading I caught myself completely lost in her, not caring if anyone noticed the wan-dering eyes of the fourth groomsman. Hopefully, the wedding guests were paying attention to Amber's crying cousin and the over-the-top poem about stars falling into the ocean.

Images flashed before me—moving pictures of how she and I arrived at this moment: bagels with vegetable cream cheese, the card table at Aunt Eileen's beach house, our first kiss after the Christmas party. My heart ached and I could feel the wetness pooling behind my eyelids. The pastor had just made some metaphor about the unbreakable bond of love, but my tears had nothing to do with the present setting and the romance playing out in front of us. Jeff and Amber were dutifully repeating their pre-scripted vows, but their voices faded to a dull murmur in my head. The bride and groom were celebrating the beginning of a life-long commitment; I stood there mourning what I was pretty sure was the unraveling of mine.

I considered the quasi-ultimatum I offered her earlier. *Was this it? Were we about to part ways because we were in different stages of life?* At that moment, Jeff must have stumbled over a word, and the crowd responded with a polite laugh. Shannon smiled in unison with everyone else, clouding my vision with a wistful jealousy. Her grin was merely a social response to the groom's miscue, but I took no joy in her amusement. *Why couldn't I be the one who made her happy?*

A sharp awareness of where we stood hit me like a misplayed line drive, taken to the head. There I was on the makeshift altar; there she was, sitting among the congregation. Suddenly, I saw Shannon clearer than ever—the skyscrapers, the folding chairs, the wedding guests framing her like a priceless piece of art—protected by glass and guarded by a velvet rope. As the rings were exchanged at sunset, it dawned on me that we were separated by much more than twenty-five feet of rooftop deck between us. There was no way I would ever be able to reach her.

It was over.

CHAPTER 32

THE MOUNTAINS WIN AGAIN

After the wedding, there was one more week of summer school at Huntington. I considered bailing and hightailing it home, but I figured the right thing to do was to stick it out. The rich kids of the Columbus suburbs weren't to blame for my broken love life; they still needed to learn how to graph functions using slope-intercept form. I presumed our hotel room quarreling would continue, but fortunately we left the ugliest of our disputes back in Chicago. I spent the remainder of my nights in Columbus sleeping on the couch, and our day-to-day living situation was bearable. Shannon and I functioned quite well as roommates, which in some way was symptomatic of our larger issues. We had no problem divvying up the long-distance calls on our phone bill, but we were incompatible when it came to the chore of creating intimacy.

On the last day of summer school, we met up one last time at Moose & Mug Coffee before treating ourselves to a nice dinner with wait staff and metal silverware. We chose an Italian restaurant we'd wanted to try, and its dim lighting and subdued atmosphere seemed to match our collective mood. When our food arrived, we ate in an uncomfortable silence, each of us perhaps considering that this was our "last supper." I had no idea what to say and didn't want to fight any more. Mercifully, Shannon initiated an innocent enough conversation.

"When do you go back to school?"

"The first day for teachers is the day after Labor Day, but I'll probably go in next week and start getting organized."

"Makes sense," she nodded and pushed some pasta around her bowl. It was my turn to ask a question.

"What are you doing tomorrow?"

"You know that girl in my class, Scarlet, I was telling you about? We were supposed to go on a hike, but it's supposed to be super-hot. So, we might go shopping instead."

Talking about the weather and schedules; this was the level to which our conversation had been downgraded. Given where we were, it was about all we could handle. The summer had stripped us bare, exposing every raw nerve and leaving us both too vulnerable to endure more pain—pain neither of us had the energy to inflict or absorb. I studied the shade of Shannon's eyes in this lighting as she continued to rearrange her cavatelli into a neat little pile.

Thoughts crossed into my head of what I could say—something profoundly insightful and personally meaningful about us and what we were experiencing—but what was the point? Anything of import had already been said. *Stick to the small talk about the weather.*

A slow slip of merlot slid past my lips, spreading warmth throughout my chest. After so much numbness, the ability to feel anything was a novel sensation. Ignoring my food and scanning the other tables at Bella Verona, I wondered what was going on in those relationships. *Was the couple by the window on the verge of getting engaged, with her anticipating it might be the night, while his sweaty hand nervously confirmed the presence of the ring box in his pocket?* I was so distracted with my made up story about Mike and Jenna (I had given them names) that Shannon had to repeat her next question.

"What time are you leaving tomorrow?"

While our dinner conversation wasn't that deep, later that evening I took part in a more meaningful dialogue, sort of. On one of my trips up and down the metal stairs, packing the car, I noted that Gladys was in her usual spot at her table. Based on the number of smashed cigarette butts in her tuna can ashtray, she had been sitting there awhile. After a half-step of hesitation, I decided to let her know about my travel plans. I crossed the courtyard and spoke before she could look up at me.

"Gladys, I'm going back to New Jersey in the morning"

"Of course, Everyone goes. No one stays. No control," she spoke into the night. It was one of the more lucid things my neighbor had ever said to me, but I wasn't convinced it was a response to what I had actually told her. Still, her string of drunken philosophical truisms landed hard on me, and I suddenly felt the weight of my circumstances. Shannon and I were no longer together, the consequence of drawing a relationship line in the sand she was unable to cross. Gladys had no idea what was going on in our upstairs apartment, yet her words were more fitting than she would ever know. My shoulders slumped and my lip stiffened.

"Good bye, Gladys."

The hand holding her cigarette moved through the air in a motion that might have been a wave; Gladys carried on narrating her nightly nonsense. My legs labored up the stairs to retrieve another batch of my belongings. When I finished packing, Shannon and I split a beer and watched the last few innings of a baseball game on TV.

In the morning, I finished loading my life into my Nissan Sentra, carefully securing the borrowed district computer and strapping my mountain bike to the back of the car with yellow bungee cords.

Shannon came down the stairs holding something behind her back.

"I think you should have this," she announced and extended the mini coffee maker.

"Are you sure? How are you going to make coffee?"

"You know me, I really don't like coffee at home, I like sugary sweet drinks with foamed milk," she said with a genuine smile. "Perhaps you can put this in your classroom."

Taking the small appliance into my hands, I recalled the day we bought it before placing it in my front seat. *The summer started with so much hope, now people are taking coffee makers back to New Jersey.*

"Well, you gave the real thing a try, huh?"

She nodded, holding back a well of inevitable tears. She threw her arms around me one last time and spoke softly and earnestly into my ear.

"I love you."

"I love you, too."

We held hands for a moment and stared at each other with the forced smiles people wear when they're breaking up. It was time to go. The last image I saw of Shannon was in my rearview mirror— her head in her hands, shoulders trembling as she sobbed, her long curls spilling over her face. *She obviously cared for me. Why couldn't she show it at other times?* My heart broke a little further knowing she had the capacity to feel so deeply about the end of our relationship while not being able to access similar depths while in it.

By the time I got to the first exit of the Pennsylvania Turnpike, the reality of our separation was starting to sink in. I wouldn't be her plus one at her sister's wedding. There would be no more Indian food and Thursday night TV. The toll booth spit out a turnpike ticket while I surveyed the menu of sixty-eight exits, mentally budgeting for the now-familiar fare for driving from Ohio to New Jersey. Shannon and I once joked on the phone that we were merely separated by the $18.75 needed to cross Pennsylvania. Now that was the price to put distance between us.

Driving east on I-76 that August morning, all I could feel was heartbreak as I approached the Allegheny Mountain Tunnel. Had I been prescient of the extended emotional storm that was on the horizon, *would I have granted her more time, patience, and grace? Maybe.* Shannon may not have loved me the way I loved her, but she did harbor me from my own overwhelming sea of grief.

Occasionally, I would glance down at the turnpike ticket and compare it to the exit signs to see how much progress I had made, mentally calculating how far I had to go. The town of Bedford was a familiar milestone, and Exit 146 meant I was about halfway home. Happiness, on the other hand, was nowhere in sight.

The concrete mouth of the tunnel swallowed me, and I descended into the earth. Beneath 250 feet of quartzite and sandstone, driving through a seemingly endless midnight, it was easy to feel insignificant. This wasn't the dim light of an Italian restaurant, but the dark shadows cast from the murkiest corners of my mind. The echoes of my engine bouncing off the corridor walls and the memories of a failed relationship merged into a steady hum of loneliness.

The brightness of day on the other side of the tunnel was no reprieve; I squinted as harsh sunlight sharply illuminated new forms and truths in my life. Refocusing my eyes, I made out a familiar face in the passenger seat; it was Grief sitting next to me, casually working on a crossword puzzle. What I didn't realize until years later was that it was always Grief—not Allie or Shannon—scripted into the final scene of this dark Hallmark movie, the one I was meant to be with all along. In a cruel twist of fate, I'd fallen in love with my own anguish and sorrow; the passenger stuck on 26-down would be my traveling companion for the foreseeable future.

Some couples have a special song for their first wedding dance; Grief and I had an entire soundtrack. As trees and billboards blurred by the window, one wistful song after another accompanied us down the highway: "Here's Where the Story Ends," "Don't Look Back in Anger," "Something's Always Wrong." It was Blues Traveler's "The Mountains Win Again" that finally brought me to tears. Midway through the harmonica solo, Grief looked up from his crossword just long enough to reach over and turn up the volume.

Allie, Shannon, the love pentagram, Columbus—all of them were distractions, misdirection as part of a larger magic trick. At the end of the illusion, the big reveal was that it only brought me back to the original hand of cards I'd been dealt: my sister had killed herself. Whether I realized it or not, I had spent the last year trying to find something good in my life, something proportional to the tragedy I'd experienced. There was no such thing.

Free of any romantic attachment, I was about to begin the long, painful process of confronting and processing the loss of my sister. And while I thought I was heading home, I was actually taking the first step of a years-long journey through misery and solitude.

What lay ahead were lonely Saturday nights marked by take-out containers, six-packs of Bud Ice, and rented movies from my local video store. I didn't even have the courage to pick out porn from the adult section behind the black curtain, opting instead for B-movies with borderline sex scenes. Phone calls from friends went unreturned. Wedding invitations would be left unopened. At a time when life should have been golf trips and Sunday brunches, I withdrew from anyone who might have cared enough to help.

And a relationship? Out of the question. I couldn't love. I couldn't be loved. Not only was I lost, I was rudderless and without a North Star. For a while, I would have to sit with myself amid the wreckage of my life.

I was alone—hopelessly alone.

www.ingramcontent.com/pod-product-compliance
Lightning Source LLC
Chambersburg PA
CBHW020135120726
47903CB00007B/2261